ESPECIALLY FOR GIRLS.

MOONSTONE ™
ROMANTIC MYSTERY

ESPECIALLY FOR GIRLS ™
presents

SOMETHING OUT THERE

LESLIE DAVIS

AN ARCHWAY PAPERBACK
Published by POCKET BOOKS • NEW YORK

For Carla Neggers who kept the faith
and Dorrie Arnold who kept the kids

This book is a presentation of
Especially for Girls™
Weekly Reader Books.

Weekly Reader Books offers book clubs for children from
preschool through high school.

For further information write to:
Weekly Reader Books
4343 Equity Drive
Columbus, Ohio 43228

Especially for Girls™
is a trademark of Weekly Reader Books.

Edited for Weekly Reader Books
and published by arrangement with
Simon & Schuster, Inc.

AN ARCHWAY PAPERBACK *Original*
This novel is a work of fiction. Names, characters, places
and incidents are either the product of the author's
imagination or are used fictitiously. Any resemblance to
actual events or locales or persons, living or dead, is
entirely coincidental.

An Archway Paperback published by
POCKET BOOKS, a division of Simon & Schuster, Inc.
1230 Avenue of the Americas, New York, N.Y. 10020

ISBN: 0-671-54451-9

AN ARCHWAY PAPERBACK and colophon are
registered trademarks of Simon & Schuster, Inc.

MOONSTONE is a trademark of Cloverdale Press.

Printed in the U.S.A.

1

"Don't forget to lock up when you leave."

Even though it was the last thing Chips Jimmerson's mother said before she left the house, the sixteen-year-old had forgotten until she was halfway down Water Street.

Let it go, just this once, she thought to herself, pushing her unruly auburn curls back from her face. She knew she'd be back in an hour to meet her sailing students anyway . . . Mrs. Porter, the housekeeper, might even get there before she did . . . and, besides, how could anything happen at ten-thirty in the morning?

But Chips knew in her heart that plenty could happen at that hour. So reluctantly she pressed her handbrakes of her ten-speed bicycle against the palms of her hands and slowly swung the bike back toward home.

The Russos and even the Wellses, the parents of her best friend Cynthia, had had robberies at their houses during the day. And as Chips's parents were always pointing out to her, the burglarized houses, like theirs, were all on the lanes off Water Street, hidden from the main road.

So back she went. As quickly as she could, Chips slid off her bike and scooted up the broad back steps of the big old New England house with the white pillars and black shutters. In less than a minute, she had pushed the button on the big brass doorknob, then, from the outside, locked the deadbolt with the key that she wore around her neck.

For good measure, she crossed the lawn to the oversized garage and pulled the heavy doors down. Though so far she hadn't heard of anyone's losing a lawn mower, she didn't want to take any chances with her sister's bike and sports equipment for every season of the year hanging on the walls.

"You can't be too careful," she said out loud, reflecting on her mother's favorite phrase. The apartment over the garage was empty, and for the first time since Chips could remember, her parents planned to rent it in September. The more people there were bustling around, they said, the less chance there would be of intruders breaking in.

A glance at her watch told Chips she'd better hurry if she wanted to be back in time to give the Bailey twins their sailing lesson. In less than fifteen minutes, she had biked her way through the quaint New England village and was standing at the counter of Nana's Homemade Ice Cream Shop.

Putting her money on the counter, she ordered gift certificates for her two nine-year-old students and a dish of butter almond ice cream for herself. Gripping her purchases tightly, she turned from the counter and bumped smack into Ryan Kennedy.

"Whoah!" the tall, seventeen-year-old boy exclaimed good-naturedly, planting his strong hands squarely on her slim shoulders. Glancing up from the dish of ice cream to his blue eyes, Chips felt her heart begin to beat wildly. The sandy-haired boy looked down at her with his eyes twinkling. His face was ruddy and his eyebrows bleached white from the sun.

"Ryan," she managed to get out, "I'm so sorry. Did I spill ice cream on your soccer uniform?"

"No harm done, Elizabeth," he broke in, slowly taking his hands from her shoulders and wiping away a few drops of ice cream. He gave her a dazzling smile as he moved around to the counter to place his order.

Chips took a seat in the deserted ice-cream parlor. Suddenly, she didn't feel hungry any more, and she watched the well-built boy in shorts and his team shirt as he waited for his ice cream. The broad green stripe across his back with a 7 in the middle was the same 7 she'd followed the entire soccer season last fall. Ryan Kennedy, the first junior ever to be named team captain, was the high school dreamboat she and her friends secretly called "Mr. Perfection."

In another hour, Nana's would be packed with the summer crowd, not only Chip's friends and other Snug Harbor locals, but also kids who came from all over the country to vacation in the picturesque seacoast village.

But at the moment, she and Ryan had the place to themselves. Chips groaned inwardly at the thought, wishing she'd worn something nicer than her cut-off jeans and her sister Melissa's faded pink polo shirt. Her sister was three years older than she, and the shirt looked it.

Taking a bite of ice cream, Chips ran her hand nervously through her curly hair. When school had let out a month ago, getting her hair cut really short had seemed like a good idea. Sailing every day made any fussy hairstyle impossible for her. Now, though, with the salty sea air frizzing it up all the more, she wasn't so sure she'd done the right thing. Darn Ryan for making her feel so self-conscious.

As she watched, he paid for his milk shake and turned in her direction. Before she could look away, he caught her eye and smiled again. "Here's to nutritious breakfasts," Ryan said, lifting his paper cup in a toast. Then, "Mind if I join you, Elizabeth?"

Chips suppressed a smile of amusement. The boy of her dreams didn't even know her well enough to realize that no one—not even her parents—called her Elizabeth. No one except Ms. Renier, their French teacher. Actually, the fact that they were both in French III was the only reason Ryan knew she was alive. And just barely at that, Chips thought, pulling the spoon out of her mouth.

"Please call me Chips, Ryan. Everybody does."

"Chips," he repeated. "I know it's your nickname. Thought maybe it was reserved for real buddies. Kinda cute."

When he sat down next to her, Chips's heart began to race again. Was he actually flirting with her? She couldn't believe it.

"My older sister couldn't say 'Elizabeth.' It came out 'Lizza-chips,' so that's what I've been for sixteen years."

Ryan laughed softly, sipping his shake. "Sixteen. How'd you get into French III? Whiz kid?"

She shook her curls, pushing away the dish of melting ice cream. "Tutors. My parents wanted us to be bilingual, so they started my sister and me in French when we were little kids. It worked. Melissa's a French major in college and she's in Paris right now. You should read her letters! She even makes going to art museums in the middle of summer sound exciting!"

Ryan nodded. "The most exciting thing to do around here is sit and wait for your house to be robbed."

"You, too?"

Ryan nodded. "Two in the afternoon. Broad daylight, can you believe it? Just like everybody else we lost silverware and my mother's jewelry, just stuff they could carry out in a hurry."

Chips shivered a little. "Was the house locked?"

"All but the garage door. They went right through there into the laundry room." Ryan frowned, crumpled up his paper cup, and tossed it neatly into a nearby trash can.

Perfect coordination, Chips thought, beginning to relax. He was surprisingly easy to talk to!

"Are you still playing soccer in July?" she asked.

"No," he replied, "I'm coaching it at Camp Cotuit every afternoon—that is, until school practice starts in August. Then I'll really have my hands full since I got elected captain again next season."

As if I didn't know, she thought, glancing at her watch. Seeing what time it had gotten to be brought her to her feet. "Gotta run myself. I teach sailing all week to kids." She held up the certificates. "Very reluctant nine-year-olds this week, so I'm going to bribe them with ice-cream cones at the end of this lesson!"

Ryan's laugh brought a smile to Chip's face as they stepped out into the parking lot. "Do you teach down at the Yacht Club?"

Chips shook her head, grabbing the handle bars of her bike in both hands. "I'm giving private lessons in my Lightning, just big enough for two kids and me. We sail off our mooring at the end of Blueberry Lane instead of out of the Yacht Club basin."

Ryan studied her for a minute, as if trying to place the spot. "The old sea captain's house with the widow's walk that looks out on Bug Light?"

When Chips nodded, he let out a low whistle, making her blush.

"We're going across the bay this afternoon," she continued. "I always end the lessons with a trip—once around the Bug Light and a picnic on Clark's Island or Outer Beach. My students this week don't live in town—they're just here for the summer—and they've never seen the lighthouse up close."

Snug Harbor Pier Lighthouse, as it was officially known, was the crusty old beacon, nearly two stories high, that had been warning mariners in stormy weather since the 1880s. It was not built on land, but on pilings driven into the rocky shoals just beneath the surface of the water at the mouth of the harbor. Constructed of rusting iron plates, the looming column was encircled by an ancient metal balcony below the room holding the light. The workings were reached by an equally rusty and precarious-looking iron staircase attached to the side. More of an eyesore than a scenic landmark, nevertheless it was beloved by everyone in town and still in use after more than a hundred years.

The Jimmerson house, along with the rest of the village, sat on the shore to the west. From there, a sandy spit of land curved out into Massachusetts Bay, forming a protective horseshoe. The weather was far from stormy now, however. The July sun was hot on Chip's shoulders as she watched Ryan get into his low-slung green sports car.

"Have a good sail," he called, then almost as an afterthought, "Chips—"

She had already pushed off on her bike and had to drag the toe of her shoe through the gravel to keep her balance.

"Hey, why don't you meet me back here tonight after your class?"

Chips felt a buzzing in her ears. Did she hear right? Was Ryan asking her for a date? He was acting so casual it was hard to tell. She struggled to seem as calm as he.

"Maybe I will," she called back offhandedly over her shoulder.

"C'mon," he yelled back. "I'll even promise to speak French. Seven-thirty?"

Chips laughed and nodded. "Okay. See you then."

With a wave that she hoped looked properly casual, she pedaled off, at breakneck speed, back toward the harbor. She felt as though she were floating as she raced the sleek tenspeed along Pilgrim Road into the village center. She even breezed up the hill past the library—a stretch that usually made her huff and puff.

Around the bend, she shifted gears, letting the offshore breeze blow back her hair. The water of the bay, off to her left, was sparkling in the late morning sun, and as the rays hit the waves, they shimmered and broke into thousands of glittery peaks. Ryan Kennedy!

Pilgrim Road ended at a fork, and with a quick glance to her left, Chips pushed onto Water Street. On either side of her, stately colonial houses with their wooden shutters and trim picket fences, shaded by ancient thick-leaved elms, blurred as she pumped the pedals. Ryan Kennedy!

That was all she could think about as she hurried along, feeling so frustrated that none of her best friends was in town right now so she could tell them she actually had a date with "Mr. Perfection." That was what bugged her about Snug Harbor. It was true that families came from near and far to vacation here but most of *her* friends tended to disappear till September. Well, she thought, now she'd really have something to write Cynthia Wells about. Cynthia had been bombarding her with postcards from her camp in Vermont, and all she ever wrote about was Jake, the tennis instructor.

The fact that their date was only going to be a rendezvous at Nana's didn't dampen Chips's excitement at all. By the time she had sped past the fish market, movie theater, and boutiques that made up the center of town, she was grinning from ear to ear.

Usually Ryan never paid any attention to underclassmen. In

fact, he'd spent most of his junior year dating Mary Thompson, who was a senior. Chips tried to imagine herself in Mary's place—waiting for Ryan after soccer practice, walking together to French . . .

The sharp blast of a car horn, sounding dangerously close to her right ear, brought Chips quickly back to reality. Just in time, she gripped the handbrakes like mad and skidded to a stop as a Jeep did the same. Her heart leaped again, but this time from fright. She had nearly run into the side of the car.

The young guy who was driving looked kind of shaken, but when he saw that she was all right, his look of concern turned to one of anger. Leaning out the open window, he glared at her. "Next time, watch where you're going, airhead," he yelled at her through clenched teeth.

Chips waited until he had turned left down the lane to the Yacht Club before she started off again—at a slower pace. He was right, no more daydreaming. By the time she turned off Water Street, the bells in the tower of the First Parish Church had just finished tolling twelve. She coasted down Blueberry Lane, past her house, bumping along the brick path that led to the boathouse at the water's edge.

The Bailey twins, already buckled into their bright orange life vests, were sitting impatiently on the dock, dangling their legs off the rough wooden boards.

"Hi, sailors!" Chips chirped brightly.

"You're late," said Amanda, scowling.

"I'm hungry," chimed in Alexander.

Chips kept smiling even though she felt like gritting her teeth. Only two lessons left, and they still hated it as much as they had the first time Mrs. Bailey deposited them on the Jimmerson dock. Acting bored as usual, they dropped down from the dock into the dinghy, making it rock precariously.

Chips took her customary seat in the stern. "Mandy, you row us out, and, Alex, you can row us back." Neither child moved. "Sit!" Chips commanded in her most authoritative tone. The twins sat.

Mandy expertly rowed the small boat out to the mooring, knowing better than to be careless once they were on the open water. Beyond them the harbor was dotted with white sails and brightly colored sailboards skimming around the channel markers. Chips smiled at the scene. She had been sailing all her life and at sixteen was one of the best instructors in the village. Once aboard the Lightning she told the twins to rig the boat, naming the parts, sails, and various lines as they did so. More groans.

Chips pulled the Nana's certificates from her pocket. The twins' faces brightened. "It's a bribe, kids. I want you to do a good job today because we're really going to test ourselves— once around Bug Light, over to the edge of the island, and home. If you pass muster, we'll do it again tomorrow and have a picnic on the island—swim and everything. Deal?"

They yipped with excitement, Mandy at the tiller, Alex handling the lines. Within half an hour they were gaily tacking back and forth across the narrow bay. The wind was light and steady, and the twins surprisingly cooperative, but Chips herself could barely concentrate. She kept seeing Ryan's face in her mind. During the next hour, she ran every word of their brief conversation through her mind a dozen times. Every time she thought about his twinkling blue eyes, she sighed.

When it was Alex's turn at the helm, she put the sail on a beam reach, letting it slide lazily out to starboard, full of wind.

"Tighten up a little . . . good boy," Chips complimented him, as she looked off toward Outer Beach. Five minutes later, she was snapped rudely back to reality by the sound of Alex's frightened voice.

"What should I do? Chips, help me!" the youngster screamed frantically. "He's too close!"

Too late, Chips looked over and realized they were on a collision course with a sailboarder. The surboardlike rig, with its bright sail billowing full out, was heading directly for their right side. With the Lightning's sail to starboard and the sailboat's to port, neither had seen the other.

In a panic, Alex shoved the tiller away, and the boat responded instantly. The wind shifted across the stern, the sail luffed, and then it billowed out rapidly on the other side.

"Duck! We're going to jibe!" was all Chips had time to yell as she grabbed the sheet from Mandy and pulled hard on the line. With a sickening *snap* the boom flew across the boat, inches above the three crouching bodies.

As the Lightning heeled dangerously to the water line, Chips threw her weight on the opposite side. The twins, too frightened to do anything but follow, tumbled over each other just in time to keep the boat from capsizing.

The sailboarder was not so lucky. To avoid smashing into them broadside, he threw his body off the board, pulling the sail with him. Almost in slow motion, the red, white, and blue nylon fell over the rider and crumpled into the water.

"We had right of way!" Chips yelled as the dripping boy pulled himself back on the board. They eyed each other in mutual surprise until the Lightning began to pull away.

"That's the second time today," the angry voice called over the water as he struggled to get back up on his sailboard. But Chips was already out of hearing range.

She turned back to the twins, expecting to find them pale with fear. To her surprise, they were glowing with excitement. "Wow," exclaimed Alex, "that's the most fun we've had all week!"

"Yeah," his sister finished, "you were great, Chips. What a heroine."

"I am *not* a heroine," Chips protested. "That never would have happened if I had been paying attention. There are two lessons we can learn from this: Avoid uncontrolled jibes, and watch the space around you. And never assume the other guy knows you have the right of way."

"But we *did* have the right of way," the twins insisted.

Chips shrugged her shoulders. "Boardsailing is so new, it's hard to say who was wrong. He should have gotten out of the way, but he didn't see us either. You can't really blame anybody."

Common sense, Chips thought to herself, should have kept her from daydreaming. To get them to calm down a little, she spent some time doing controlled jibes, showing the twins they had nothing to fear under the right circumstances. Soon they were at the mouth of the harbor, with Bug Light looming from its perch atop the shoals off the island.

For a boat as small as the Lightning, sailing around the light at high tide was easy. Chips gave both kids a chance at the tiller as they approached. All three of them stared up at the rusted sides of the conical structure looming above them, craning to see the glassed beacon inside the iron railing. Sea gulls, insulted by their arrival, flew in every direction, screeching and wheeling through the air. *What a nautical scene,* Chips thought, watching the water lap at the ladder.

"Jeez," said Alex, "it's a *lot* bigger than I thought. Sure doesn't look like a bug out here."

"Not from here," Chips repeated, "but from the shore it's just a spot. Did you two know my house was built for a sea captain? The little balcony around the peak on the roof is called a 'widow's walk.' It was built so the wives of sailors could watch for the ships as they came into the harbor right here. Of course, that was long before the lighthouse was built."

"Yeah," murmured Mandy, "I bet that was back in the days when pirates would swoop down on you, right out there." As she pointed to the island, Alex gave her a jab in the padded vest.

"Don't start telling any of your dumb pirate stories," he warned his sister.

Chips laughed as they rounded the light, skimming easily between it and the pine-covered land now off the starboard. Once safely through the narrows, she gave the tiller back to Mandy as they coasted along the shore of the island. Together they looked for clear spots for the next day's picnic.

"Over there," shouted Alex, pointing to a sandy clearing. Chips was following the direction of her student's finger when the sharp whine of an outboard motor broke the silence. At first, nothing was visible but the rising from the island of more sea gulls, disturbed by the noise. They called to one another shrilly as they left the pines, joining the birds circling the lighthouse behind them.

Chips's hand tightened over Mandy's on the long wooden tiller, her eyes squinting in the direction of the sound. The twins, always eager for adventure, followed her glance, waiting with her.

From a cove just ahead, a small motorboat in high gear raced out into the open water, its wake slapping the small sailboat broadside. The Lightning began to rock as though they were jibbing again, making the twins grip the sides.

Chips was used to being bothered by motorboats. She knew a few obnoxious kids who got their kicks out of buzzing around the bay, circling her or her friends, and churning up waves that pitched the sailboats up and down precariously. Harmless—but pesty—behavior.

But this skipper was no joy-riding teenager, and the look on his face told her he meant business. A scuffy-looking man about ten years older than she stood at the wheel. Even under the broiling midsummer sun, he was dressed in a blue-jean jacket. He turned suddenly in their direction, coming so close she could see what looked like a three days' growth of beard on his jaw and a bulky diving watch on his wrist. There was something menacing about him, and Chips shivered without knowing why.

"Hey," yelled Mandy, imitating her teacher. "We've got right of way!"

Chips grabbed the child's shoulder, pushing her into a sitting position. "Hush," she hissed, "both of you." The twins, sensing her concern, were suddenly still.

As quickly as he had appeared, he was gone, flying past them into the channel. They all watched as he headed past the light and south toward Plymouth, the next town on the coast. It was Alex who broke the silence.

"We *did* have right of way, didn't we?"

Chips looked at both of them as she pulled the sail back in. "I don't think it mattered much to him," she muttered. "I have half a mind to report him to the harbor master. Mr. Ransome always wants to know about creeps like that."

"Yeah," added Alex, "especially since he didn't have any registration numbers."

A sudden chill shot through Chips as she looked at Alex in alarm. "Are you sure?" she asked.

"Yup," he answered. "Right where Dad has ours on the bow, that guy's were painted out. I saw it, black streaks. Gee, maybe he *is* a pirate. Wow. Let's look for treasure on the island tomorrow."

"Now who's acting creepy?" his twin asked, looking over into the deep piney woods of Clark's Island.

The kids continued their pirate conversation, oblivious of Chips's worried look. Suddenly she was grateful for the daylight and the presence of other boats in the bay, even if they were far beyond calling range. She'd had more than enough excitement for one day. As she let out the sail to return before the wind, she brought the twins' attention back to naming the parts of the boat.

Back at the Jimmerson mooring, the three of them busied themselves stowing the sail and neatly coiling the sheet, halyards, and other lines.

"Well," Chips finally said, trying to sound cheerful, "maybe we should finish the lessons tomorrow with a picnic and swim right here. Or, if you're extra good, I'll take you to the Yacht Club . . ."

Identical wails arose from the twins before she could go any farther.

"Aw, come on. It'll be *sooo* exciting to go back there," Mandy exclaimed.

"You promised, Chips. Like, you're not scared of that skuzzy guy, are you?" Alex looked from his teacher to his sister, his face lighting up at the thought of danger.

"No, I'm not." Chips laughed, shrugging off her uneasiness. *I am being silly,* she thought to herself. "Okay, you little monsters, a deal's a deal."

The day ended brightly as the twins clambered up onto the pier, hung their life vests in the boathouse, and mounted their bikes for the quick ride home. After extracting solemn promises from them to be on time the next day, Chips waved good-bye and started up toward her house.

The handsome white colonial with its black shutters and cheery window boxes sat back from the water, facing out to sea. It was like a picture postcard of New England, with an old apple orchard beyond the boathouse and a graceful lawn sloping from the big front door down to the water. The Jimmersons' closest neighbors lived in houses on the corner of the village street and Blueberry Lane. Even those two houses were hidden from view by neat rows of privet.

Suddenly she heard a motor. It sounded like the family lawn mower, and Chips thought for a moment that her father had come home early. But then she remembered that it was Thursday night and Dr. Jimmerson had surgery scheduled. Her mother wouldn't be home either—she had a hospital board meeting.

Because both of her parents worked, the three of them—with the help of their housekeeper, Alice Porter—always made sure they checked with each other about their schedules on a weekly basis. Chips was given a great deal of independence, a responsibility she took seriously. She was proud of the fact that her busy parents felt they could count on her and trusted her judgment. She was thinking how much she wanted to tell them about Ryan, when the mower and its rider came into view from behind the garage.

"What are *you* doing on my lawn mower?" Chips shouted over the roaring engine.

"Trying for the third time not to hit you!" he exclaimed, letting go of the brake. Ignoring Chips's dirty look, the agile driver who had nearly run her over with his Jeep and nearly collided with her on his sailboard continued on the machine out into the front lawn.

Chips noticed that his thick brown hair was still wet from the bay. He had broad shoulders, and she could see the muscles of his back ripple under his sweat-stained T-shirt as he maneuvered the lawn mower around the flower beds.

For once in her life Chips was speechless.

2

With a determined twist, she dug her Topsiders into the grass and marched toward the back door. As Chips had hoped, Mrs. Porter was still there, putting together a shrimp salad for her dinner.

"*Who* hired that guy to do our lawn?" Chips felt a little sheepish as the housekeeper turned from her spot at the kitchen counter to give her young charge a sharp look.

"What happened to 'Hi, Mrs. Porter, I'm home?' " the older woman asked with a twinkle in her eye.

"I'm sorry," Chips apologized, giving her a hug. "I was so surprised to see him out there . . ."

She followed Alice Porter's pointing finger to the tidy desk in the corner, and picked up a check made out to Jeffrey Taylor. Beneath it was a printed business card which read:

Jeffrey Taylor
Lawn Care, House-Sitting, Maintenance
Odd Jobs

22 Colony Drive   585-9957

"Your father was looking for someone to take over the lawn, help around the house . . . you know, odd jobs, just like it says." Mrs. Porter washed her hands, patting them dry with the dish towel. "*I* checked his references myself. He does the Wellses' yard, Russos', too. Comes highly recommended. If I know Dr. Jimmerson, he wants the place to look busy and occupied, especially when he and your mother are at the medical convention."

Chips looked from the card back to the housekeeper. "You don't mean Dad's hired him to house-sit! You and I will be here. Besides, he doesn't look any older than I do."

Mrs. Porter was smiling with amusement. "You are putting

up an awfully big argument, young lady. You know I'm only here part-time, in the daytime at that. And with my sister in the hospital, I can't give you all the attention you need."

Chips made a face at the implication that she needed a sitter. She would rather have stayed with another family during her parents' absence, but she knew it was the house they were thinking of.

"Do you know this fellow?" Mrs. Porter asked as she watched Chips put the card back on the desk.

"No. I bumped into him a few times today, that's all." . . . *and made a complete klutz of myself,* she added silently.

Twenty minutes later, Mrs. Porter had said good-bye for the day and locked up. With less than an hour until she left for her date, Chips let her mind wander back to Ryan.

Her reverie made her miss Melissa more than ever. She had gotten used to her older sister's absence during the school year, but the summer in France had been a last-minute invitation, one that left Chips painfully aware of how much she depended on Melissa's advice and encouragement.

She took a quick shower, which refreshed her, but as she stepped from the bathroom that connected her room with Melissa's, the sound of the lawnmower made her frown. *If Melissa were here, Jeffrey Taylor, whoever he was, would not have been hired to house-sit. She and I could have handled things just fine.*

The two sisters had the front bedrooms which looked out over the bay, a view that seemed breathtaking to Chips ever time she looked out on the water. The girls' parents, who had sacrificed the sea view for one of the orchards along the side, had a master suite—bedroom, sitting room/office, and bath.

A guest room completed the fourth corner of the main section, although the back stairs came up into a hallway with two more rooms and a bath. Originally for servants, one was now used for sewing and crafts, the other for out-of-season clothes.

As Chips surveyed her wardrobe, she felt butterflies gathering in her stomach. What should she wear? She didn't want Ryan to think she was too anxious, or that she even considered this a real date. Finally she pulled on a pair of fresh khaki shorts and a lime green T-shirt. They fit her well and were far more flattering than the cut-offs and polo shirt of the morning. Intending to walk to Nana's, she traded in her boating shoes for green espadrilles, which matched her shirt. She didn't want to take either her bike or the car, in case Ryan offered to drive her home.

Downstairs Chips devoured her dinner and left a note for her parents telling them she would be meeting "a new friend, Ryan Kennedy," at Nana's and would be home early. She left it on their regular spot, the corner of the kitchen desk. Jeffrey Taylor's check was still sitting there, so she picked it up before scooting out into the evening light.

Jeff was walking up from the garage, pushing a ten-speed racing bike, as Chips let the door slam behind her.

"I guess this is for you," she said, holding out the check. For a moment, he stood looking into her eyes, long enough for Chips to notice that his were a deep brown, the same shade as his thick, now-dry hair.

"Thanks," was all he said as he folded it, sliding the paper into his jeans.

Chips left him on the lawn and headed out toward Blueberry Lane. She wanted to walk in peace, and, as far as she was concerned, the sooner she was out on Water Street, the better. No such luck. Before she had gone fifty feet, she heard the crunch of bicycle tires behind her. She didn't miss a step, though, as Jeffrey fell in beside her, pushing his bike.

"So *you* turn out to be Chips Jimmerson, famous helmsman. Or should I say helmswoman. Mrs. Porter was telling me all about you and your sailing classes this afternoon. You can imagine my surprise when the expert instructor she was talking about turned out to be you."

Chips felt her face burn, horrified to discover that this stranger could make her blush. "At least I know the rules of the road," she replied, still looking straight ahead. "I had the right of way."

"On the bay or on Water Street?"

Chips spun around to face him, her eyes blazing, but before

she could think of anything to say he took her hand and shook it. "I'm Jeff Taylor and you've been giving me that look all day."

She dropped his hand and resumed her walk, feeling just a tiny bit curious that he didn't look at all familiar to her. She, however, was not about to give him the satisfaction of asking anything personal as whether he was new in town. "I know who you are, thank you. Now if you'll excuse me, I'm trying to meet a friend."

They had reached the main road and, as Chips started along the sidewalk, Jeff hopped on his bike, balancing with one Docksider shoe along the curb. "Date?"

"Yes," she half-lied, hoping to get rid of him. "I'm meeting Ryan Kennedy at Nana's."

"Ryan Kennedy," Jeff repeated as though he'd never heard the name. "Does he sail, too?"

"Not that I know of. He's captain of the soccer team," she finished in a huff. *How could anyone not know Ryan?* she thought in disgust.

"Doesn't sail, doesn't even pick you up at your house. Poor kid's gotta walk across town to meet him. Some date." The more he joked, the angrier Chips got—both at Jeff and at herself for letting his teasing bother her.

Then unexpectedly, he pushed off the curb.

"Have a good time with your soccer star. See you around the water, Chips Jimmerson."

Feeling strangely disconcerted, Chips stared at the retreating figure for a moment before she continued on toward the ice-cream parlor.

Summer evenings were cool in Snug Harbor and very quiet. Teenagers made their own fun, which usually meant a movie, Nana's, or the beach. Chips waved to a few familiar faces outside the Bayside Cinema across the street. Another half block: the Sou'wester Book Shop, Dockside Clothier, and the post office, and she again was passing through a residential area.

Snug Harbor was her hometown, her father's and grandfather's. With one or two exceptions she knew the families in each of the big colonial houses along her path. Here and there, lights were coming on, but it was Thursday, mid-July, and even at 7:15, lawn mowers still buzzed, and children called from the wide back yards. Chips nearly skipped along the sidewalk, thinking of Ryan's deep-blue eyes.

She didn't pay attention to the passing cars until a battered sedan stopped ahead of her, the red brake lights shining. As she approached, Chips could see the driver slide over to the passenger window. It was obvious he wanted to talk with her, but when Chips got closer, her throat tightened in surprise.

It was the skipper from the unregistered boat. Her glance fell to his diving watch as he pointed his finger at her.

"Harbor master know you're nosing around the light?"

Her fear melted to anger at his rudeness, and she wanted to tell the scruffy stranger it was none of his business. Instead Chips shoved her fists into her pockets and raised her voice so she wouldn't have to step any closer.

"I teach sailing and take my students out around the light at the end of each week. "I'm very careful."

"Tides can be treacherous out there," he broke in.

Chips was startled by his concern. "I know. We're only out there when the tide's coming in. Wouldn't want to be swept out to sea," she finished lightly.

"Follow my advice, and stay back in the basin. It ain't safe." As abruptly as he had started, the skipper stopped, pulled his head back in the car, and took off.

For a moment, Chips felt as though she were rooted to the sidewalk. A knot formed in her stomach, and her breath came in little gasps until she leaned against the fence for support. *It's nothing,* she told herself, *just some guy who doesn't know what a good sailor I am.*

"Friend of yours?"

Spinning around at the sound of a voice behind her, Chips found Jeff Taylor again, propped on his bicycle, his foot on the curbstone. When he saw how pale her face was, his grin turned to a look of concern.

"Hey," he said softly, "who was that guy?"

Chips swallowed and shook her head. "Nobody. Just somebody concerned about my sailing. Never mind, Jeffrey." Abruptly she started off again, determined not to do anything to provoke his teasing.

"You get in *his* way, too, this afternoon?"

She kept on walking, not bothering to turn toward him with an answer. He was impossible!

"Whatever you say, sailor," he quipped lightly, preparing to push off. "So long. Have fun with Brian."

"*Ryan,*" she corrected him with annoyance she made no attempt to hide, "Ryan Kennedy."

"Right," he added, "soccer captain," and pedaled off into the dusk.

Though the ice-cream shop was just ahead, the walk suddenly seemed endless. The daylight was faded, leaving eerie shadows all around her, and Chips found herself wishing Jeff hadn't taken off so quickly. By the time Nana's brightly lighted front porch came in view, Chips was ready to run the remaining distance.

She spotted Ryan sitting outside with a group of friends, and her heart warmed.

Chips watched him get to his feet as she approached, thinking he looked even more handsome than he had that morning in his fresh jeans and blue turtleneck jersey. They talked for a minute and then, with his hand pressed gently against her back, he ushered her through the screen door.

"Another butter almond?" he asked as they reached the counter.

He remembered, she thought with a sigh, feeling good when she saw all the faces turned in their direction. Chips Jimmerson with Ryan Kennedy—it would be all over town by morning. When the sundaes were ordered, he pointed to an empty table for two in the corner, much to her surprise.

"Let's sit over here where we can hear ourselves think," he said.

Once they were by themselves, she coaxed him to talk about his day, feeling thrilled as she listened to his easy laughter in between his anecdotes about teaching soccer to little kids.

"If they kicked the ball as much as they kick each other, we might make it to the goalposts more than once an hour." Halfway through a story he stopped cold, however, looking into her troubled face.

"You're a million miles away, Chips. What's up?"

"I'm sorry," she said, shaking her head. "Nothing much, just a creepy set of circumstances." Yet when she told him about the twins and the sinister skipper in the unregistered boat, the story sounded silly to her, and she wound up just shrugging her shoulders.

"I don't think I would have thought much about it if he hadn't stopped me in the street on the way over here."

Ryan looked surprised, but when she finished, he nodded his head in agreement. "I don't sail, but I've been around outboard motorboats enough to know he's right about the tide—the lighthouse, too, for that matter. He probably thinks you're a reckless kid and he's doing you a favor. Say," he finished, "why don't you take me out there, give me a couple of lessons so I can see for myself?"

"I'd love to," she said easily, trying not to show that his suggestion was the most exciting thing that had happened to her all week. "Saturday morning about nine the tide will be right."

He wrinkled his nose at the hour, making her laugh. "You'll manage," she cracked.

Finishing their ice cream, they talked awhile longer and then dropped their dishes in the trash bins on the way back outside. Half a dozen friends, some his, some hers, spoke to them as they wound their way through the tables.

"Hey, Ryan, Chips. Catch you later at the party?"

"It's early. I told the gang we'd meet them at the beach," Ryan said, pointing to the empty benches to show her that a lot of the kids had gone on ahead.

Chips tried not to look disappointed. "I can't. My parents aren't home and I left them a note saying I'd be back early."

He shrugged. "No problem. I'll drive you home and you can change the note."

"I can't do that, Ryan," she replied, wishing with all her heart that she could. "To stay out that late, I'd have to clear it with them first. That's only fair."

"Fair," he repeated a little too sarcastically. "Do you have to tell them where you are every minute?"

Chips didn't like his tone or the way he tried to make her feel inexperienced. She looked up into his face. "When my mother decided to go back to work, we all agreed that she should always know where I am. We run the family on the honor system. They both happen to be out tonight, so I should be home early. The reason I get as much independence as I do is 'cause they *know* they can trust me."

Ryan didn't say anything for a minute, which made Chips feel as though she'd spoiled the evening. "And I suppose you know exactly where they are?"

"Sure," she replied. "Dad's in surgery at Plymouth General Hospital and Mom's at a board meeting. She works full-time as Director of Volunteer Services, and she's presenting a report tonight."

Suddenly Ryan laughed, yanking the jersey out of his jeans to show Chips a small scar on his abdomen. "Dr. Jimmerson! He took out my appendix. What do you know!" His dreamy blue eyes shone down at her, amused. "I guess we can't have Doctor Jimmerson so worried about where his daughter is that he can't operate."

"Thanks for understanding," she said—though she wasn't entirely sure that he did.

Ryan put his arm lightly around her shoulders, which made her pulse race. "I think I'd better drive you home—to protect you from mysterious skippers."

"Ryan—"

The ride back to Blueberry Lane went by far too quickly. Before Chips knew it, Ryan had swung his car into the drive, and was letting the engine idle as she got out of the car. He caught up with her in front of the door as she turned to say good-bye.

The headlights cast long, distorted shadows onto the lawn, and it felt good to move in closer to him.

"See you here Saturday," he said, giving her hand a little squeeze.

She nodded, her heart racing at his touch, and unlocked the door. "Thanks for the ice cream. I guess you're going out to the beach?"

"Yup," he answered, "but it's not too late to change your mind."

"I can't."

"Okay. You'll be missed." As quickly as he had said it, he brushed her lips in a half kiss and headed for the car. It was several minutes before she moved from her spot against the door. As she locked the door and raced up the back stairs two at a time, a big grin spread over her face.

A single lamp glowed on the hall table upstairs; set on a timer, it flicked on automatically at dusk. Through the screened windows, Chips heard First Parish's bells tolling eleven. As the ringing stopped, it was replaced by the faint, froggy blast of Bug Light's horn. *Heavy weather coming in,* Chips thought.

She was about to head for her own room when she paused, deep in thought. Turning on her heels, she went back to the attic door at the back stairs landing. Snapping on the bare overhead light, Chips moved quickly up the stairs.

Dr. Jimmerson was an astronomy buff, and he had tried for years to get his family interested in the stars. While neither of his daughters shared his enthusiasm, both were familiar with the fine telescope he kept near the widow's walk.

Chips opened the door leading out to the fenced-in space along the roof. Taking the instrument with her, she set it down on the terrace. When it was in place she flicked off the light and turned to face the water. The night air was foggy this close to the bay. Moving up to the eyepiece, Chips turned the focusing knob to bring Bug Light into view. Nothing. It was too dark and too misty to see anything. Again she adjusted the refracting lens, grateful that the image—if she found one—would be right side up. Her father's first telescope reflected everything upside down. It was no wonder she couldn't tell the Big Dipper from Orion!

She was smiling to herself when the lighthouse came into view, flooded by the flash of its beacon. With the scene magnified at 150 power, Chips could immediately tell what she was looking at. Like a flashbulb in a camera, the light swung right at her, illuminating the west side of the rusty balcony. There was the ladder, the tip of the cement column, towering above the shoals, and then a smaller, bobbing light below. Darkness.

But light flashed again, then she lost it. Moving the lens to her left, her eye strained to pick up the spot. She waited. Then she saw it. A light flickering, bouncing on the water. Was it a boat, she wondered? Maybe lobstermen checking the pots anchored randomly across the channel. It was impossible to tell.

She tried to imagine Ryan and his friends out partying on a motor boat, but decided her imagination was working overtime. In her mind's eye she saw the skipper again, roaring out of the pines at them, sea gulls screeching in his wake.

Gooseflesh, like a thousand tiny spiders creeping up her arm, made her push the telescope away. Chips put the instrument in its upright position, but before she could turn to the attic, a hand grabbed her shoulders. A scream tore from her throat, reverberating with the fog horn, in the heavy night air.

3

Before she could catch her breath, Chips was pulled anxiously into a hug, one that felt familiar.

"Chips, darling!"

"Daddy," she moaned gratefully. "You scared me to death!"

Dr. Jimmerson's expression was a mixture of amusement and concern. "Your note is still down on the kitchen desk, so your mother and I thought you were still out. Then, when I saw the attic door open . . ."

"You thought I was a thief up here ransacking the attic," she finished for him.

Her father laughed. "You gave us quite a scare." Together they returned the telescope to its resting place, and when Paul Jimmerson spoke again, his voice was hopeful. "Finally taking an interest in astronomy?"

Chips shrugged her shoulders. "Not exactly. I was looking at Bug Light. I took the Bailey twins around it today and all of a sudden a guy in a motorboat came flying out of the inlet on the island, out of Pilgrim Cove. I came up here to look, and I swear I saw lights right where that guy was." She shrugged. "I'm probably letting my imagination run away with me. Ryan thinks so, anyway."

Her father closed the attic door as they went down to the second floor. "You may be right. It was a fabulous camping spot thirty years ago. Secluded from view . . . great for getting into trouble, I might add."

Chips thought about the incident last summer when her father found beer cans and cigarettes in their little motorboat after Melissa had taken it across the bay to a clambake. But she'd gone to Outer Beach. *Certainly,* Chips thought, *if anyone partied at Pilgrim Cove, I'd know about it . . . or Ryan would.*

Her mother came to the bedroom door. "How was your evening at Nana's?"

Chips's smile got broader, even though she tried to look nonchalant as she paused a few minutes before telling them about the soccer captain. "You'll like him," she finished. "Everybody likes Ryan Kennedy."

She walked down the hall and had nearly gotten to her own room when her father called her back. "Have you had a chance to meet the Taylor fellow?"

Pop! Like a pin in a balloon, the lighter-than-air feelings about Ryan disappeared. "We met," she answered curtly, "while he was mowing the lawn." She couldn't see any reason to add that she had nearly run him over twice in a single afternoon, and that his teasing convinced her that he thought she *was* a complete klutz.

"Wonderful," Chip's mother was saying, oblivious of the put-out look on her daughter's face. "He'll be staying over the garage while we're in Denver at the medical convention. He comes highly recommended."

"I don't need a baby-sitter."

Mrs. Jimmerson opened her eyes wider. "My goodness, Chips. Of course you don't. We didn't hire Jeffrey to baby-sit. We simply need someone to look after the house, keep it looking occupied."

"Look at what just happened tonight," her father added. "I scared the daylights out of you simply by coming up to the attic. The whole town's on edge, and Jeff is just what we need for the few days we'll be gone—a little insurance, you might say."

"*You* might," she muttered.

"Besides," Anne Jimmerson was chirping, "he intends to study landscape architecture, and he's looking for gardens to work on. Heaven knows, this old property needs a lot of attention. Frankly, I think he was delighted to get the job. He's anxious to earn money."

It was useless to argue with two adults who were making it clear that as far as they were concerned, Jeffrey Taylor had dropped out of heaven to solve all their problems. Nevertheless, Chips gave it her best shot.

"Mrs. Porter and I can manage fine, you know."

"Alice can only stay during the day because of her sister," her dad said. "Besides, I like the idea of a man's being around."

Chips rolled her eyes toward the ceiling. "Come on," she moaned, "you're surrounded by women. Melissa and me and Mom and Mrs. Porter . . . we've always done just fine, and besides, your landscape *man* doesn't look any older than I am."

"I will be halfway across the country and the women you just named will be reduced by half, Chips," replied her father, but it was her mother who gave her the thoughtful look.

"He's eighteen. That is rather close to your age. Frankly, Chips, darling, you've always been such a tomboy, I never gave a thought to this bothering you. Have you developed a crush on him?"

"You are *so* hopeless!" Chips muttered, shaking her head vehemently. She just wished her parents didn't always sound like they were from another century. "I do not have a 'crush' on him. Believe me."

"The subject is closed, anyway," her father added. The Taylor boy has done this for the Russos, and he comes highly recommended."

"They were robbed, you know," Chips couldn't help adding.

"That was after Jeffrey had left. As a matter of fact, this gives you that freedom you keep talking about. With him here, you just may come and go as you normally would. You won't have to worry about the house, and you may see your friends as much as you want, you don't have to have a thing to do with him."

Chips nodded, knowing defeat when it stared her in the face. Her parents were right about one thing, anyway. She intended to concentrate on Ryan and have nothing to do with the would-be landscape architect/house-sitter.

They ended the night with smiles and when Chips finally scooted under her sheets, she lay still listening to the faint honking of Bud Light's fog horn. Pilgrim Cove—she'd have to ask Ryan about it on Saturday.

Ryan will know, she repeated to herself dreamily, falling asleep as she thought about his twinkling blue eyes.

*   *   *

Chips's parents decided to let her sleep late, so by the time she had gotten dressed and down to the kitchen at nine, they were gone. Alice Porter, however, was back, happily agreeing to pack a picnic lunch for the Clark's Island outing.

When the Bailey twins rode their bicycles down Blueberry Lane, Chips was already waiting at the end of the dock, wicker hamper stocked with sandwiches, punch, and the famous Porter chocolate-chip cookies beside her.

"You remembered," Mandy cried gleefully, clapping her hands.

"This'll be the best part," her brother added, tightening the straps of his life jacket.

"It's a reward for a perfect sail," Chips added with a smile, as the twins moaned in unison and lowered themselves into the dinghy.

"Come on, you're old pros by this time."

Mandy was nodding in agreement. "After yesterday we can handle anything. I sure hope we run into someone today—jibbing is the best!" She missed Chips's troubled look as she lifted her chubby hand to shade her eyes, scanning the harbor.

"Jibbing is just changing directions, and you can do it without running into *anybody*," Chips replied sourly, instructing them to rig the boat.

Once they were under sail, the twins worked enthusiastically to impress their captain. Alex pointed to the triangular sail. "Marconi rig, head, tack, clew on each of the corners."

"Outhaul," Mandy added, touching the cleated end of the line at the wooden boom, "downhaul, halyard, and sheaves."

Chips threw up her arms, laughing. "Perfect," she cried. "Did you two stay up all night memorizing?"

They looked at each other. "We'd do anything for Mrs. Porter's chocolate-chip cookies on Clark's Island. Your house is to starboard, on the right," Mandy broke in with a grin, "and the boardsailor's to port! There he is, Chips, the red, white, and blue one way over there."

As if I didn't know which one she meant, Chips thought, following Mandy's pointing finger to the agile form of Jeffrey Taylor running his sailboard out between the island and Outer Beach.

He was far enough away to be out of earshot, but Mandy started yelling "you-whoooooo, youuuuuuuuu-who," repeatedly until Chips yanked her into the cockpit by the hem of her life jacket.

"Let him concentrate, for heaven's sake," she muttered as the sail mixed with half a dozen other brightly colored ones.

For once, the youngsters cooperated and dutifully returned to their tasks. They sailed in a leisurely way, gently tacking across the bay as they worked their way out to the mouth of the harbor. The mist, heavy enough to warrant the fog horn last night, was burning off rapidly, leaving only blue sky above them and a light breeze riffling the waves.

As they drew closer to their destination, Chips tried to ignore the knotting in her stomach. Tension made her edgy as the crusty old beacon loomed closer and closer and two nine-year-olds looked up in awe, their mouths agape.

Chips took the helm, letting them study the landmark. Here and there brightly colored markers bobbed in the waves to mark where lobster pots lay below waiting to trap the elusive crustaceans. Chips was careful to give them a wide berth. Pleasure boats were the bane of the lobsterman's existence, since if the sailor fouled the lines the pot might have to be cut free and the catch lost.

An angry lobsterman is all I need, Chips thought as they came around the beacon and she gave the tiller to Alex. She kept her hand over the child's, watching as both twins beamed with pride at their skills.

"Good work . . . Mandy, tighten the sail a little . . . the wind will shift here . . . Alex, let it out some . . ." The rocks so close to the surface at low tide were now well-submerged, and the kids came around the lighthouse like professionals.

Chips clapped her hands, giving them both an ovation, proud of her students and proud of herself for finally getting some enthusiasm from them.

She took a minute to shield her eyes and look up at the rusting relic, squinting at the railing. Scores of sea gulls screeched in protest as the Lightning disturbed their peace, launching themselves out into the windstream above the little boat. She looked hard at the middle rung of the ladder running up the side.

"Kids," Chips said suddenly, "come about and head back for a minute."

"You promised!"

"We're almost there!"

"Hush," she commanded sharply. "I just want to give you one more chance to practice a jibe," she fibbed, still staring at the spot on the ladder.

The padded orange vests bumped and scrambled back into position as Alex muttered, "Aye, aye, Captain," under his breath and maneuvered the Lightning into a perfectly executed jibe.

"You don't have to be so tough. We're only nine, you know," Mandy whined. Chips gave her a moment's attention. "Then you may come about instead."

That made her happy, and Chips had a chance to confirm what she had suspected. One gull was not real. It was a sea gull decoy, a perfect replica of the live ones, and it sat propped up among the others on the middle rung of the ladder!

*　　*　　*

While Alex hauled up the centerboard, Mandy let the Lightning slide gently onto the sandy bottom by the clearing Chips had spotted. A cinder block beneath the surface became the anchor, and as she moored the boat, she wondered how long ago someone else had put it there for the same purpose.

With considerable effort she put the decoy out of her mind and concentrated on enjoying the sun and sandwiches. The discarded life vests served as cushions, and, while Chips took a sunbath, Alex and Mandy scurried up and down the beach collecting shells and dead horseshoe crabs. The shells they could keep; the crabs, Chips informed them, had to go.

"Only if we can bring home more shells instead," Alex bartered. Reluctantly agreeing, Chips got to her feet and brushed the sand off her legs, stretching her sun-warmed body contentedly.

Dragging her canvas beach bag, Mandy led the way along the sandy edge of the island. When you looked at it from high atop the Jimmersons' widow's walk, Clark's Island was a neat blob of land, rising from the water like an enormous sea creature. As children Chips and Melissa had often argued about whether it looked more like a giant whale or a hippopotomus wallowing at the mouth of the harbor.

In all the years she had lived in town, Chips had never explored more than the edges of this piece of land. Near the beach grew beach plums, and father back little scrub pines had taken hold in the sandy soil. Thick, overgrown trees blanketed the spine of the island so densely that she doubted that sunlight ever made it to the forest floor.

But in all those years, it had never occurred to her to be afraid out here. Not that she was now, she quickly told herself—just a little wary of those hidden inlets and coves like the one the skipper had flown out of.

Now, under the hot sun, the little band followed the rim of sand along the water. Around the bend, the beach widened and then opened sharply into a watery inlet, the salt water slicing through the beach plum and pines like a hidden river.

Pilgrim Cove, Chips thought to herself. Alex went splashing right into the shallow inlet and promptly sank up to his ankles in mud. "Oh, gross!" he yelled at the top of his lungs. Chips sent him wading out into the bay to wash off his shoes and took that moment to pause and look out across the water towards the Jimmerson house.

There was no doubt in her mind that this was the spot she had sighted in the telescope the night before. Barely visible from the far point of land where she lived, it was hidden completely from the town farther in along the basin. No wonder kids liked it. Shallow, protected, it was perfect for camping and beach parties.

The twins headed back in her direction, inventing scary stories about pirates and trying to follow each other's footprints in the sand as Chips continued ahead, along the edge of the land. It rose sharply on the backside of the island, the water lapping below the overhanging beach-plum blossoms.

"Let's climb the cliffs and find a lookout," Alex challenged his sister, and before Chips could stop them, they wriggled their way through the brush and started to climb. The path, such as it was, was scratchy and overgrown with low branches, and by the time Chips had worked her way through to the top, the twins were already perched on the edge of the sandy cliff, looking across at Outer Beach and down at the wet sand below them.

She knelt beside them, letting her gaze drop to the water lapping the shore. Suddenly a silent sweeping motion made her gasp. She could not have been more surprised if the fin of a shark had glided by, but Jeffrey Taylor was no shark. Just as silently, the red tip of his sail moved out from the pines below them as he walked the board into knee-deep water.

"Be quiet," she hissed to the twins, and they sat like little spies peering down at him as he eased the board into the wind and caught the breeze. They were close enough so that Chips could see the muscles in his tanned back ripple as he pulled on the boom and steadied himself. She found herself begrudgingly admiring the skill with which he handled the board, moving gracefully among the shoals, skimming the shore. But what in the world was he doing on this island?

Watched by unseen eyes, Jeff worked the board along two tacks, picking up speed until he was clear of the island and too far out to be seen clearly any more. She wondered if he resented the fact that he had to tend the Jimmerson gardens instead of being able to sail more. He must really need the money to be working so hard for so many families during the summer.

The twins had left their vantage point and were pushing their way back through the undergrowth. When Chips caught up with them, they were sticking their shoes into the inlet. "Let's follow it, Chips," Mandy whispered. "Maybe there's a pirate's hideout back in there."

Before Chips could protest, her two independent charges were marching along the tidal flow. As she watched them scurrying ahead of her on their chubby legs, the glint of sunlight bounced off something and caught her eye. Ahead in a stand of pines, the stern of a boat peeked from a low patch of beach plum.

There was no mistaking the boat. Though there were lots of

them like it in the area, Chips knew immediately that it was the skipper's. And as if she needed proof, Mandy started crying with delight, "Hey, look! The pirate's boat is hidden right here!"

Chips knew it was hopeless to yell at Mandy to be quiet, so she leveled a look at her that said *Another word and you're in BIG trouble.* Much to her relief, it seemed to do the trick, Mandy's eyes grew round and her voice dropped to a stage whisper. "He might be right around here waiting for us."

"Yes, he might," Chips hissed back, "and he would probably like nothing better than to feed you to the sea gulls!"

"Oh, wow," her brother added.

"Piece by piece," Chips threw in for effect.

For all her joking and the kids' cockeyed sense of adventure, Chips felt far from lighthearted. Instead she felt a sense of alarm, which she tried to hide as she fought an urge to shake the twins and run with them back to the Lightning.

She turned her attention to the boat. "Hardly shipshape, guys. I hope you'll never leave your lines in a mess like this."

To satisfy their curiosity, Chips let them peer into the cockpit at the tangle of cording, bobbers, and lobster pots thrown randomly into the boat. The skipper's bobbers were painted with green and yellow stripes, and though Chips tried to remember if she'd ever seen his colors around the lighthouse waters, she couldn't recall.

"Geez," Alex was whining, "I guess he isn't much of a pirate after all, just an old lobsterman."

"Some adventure," Mandy added.

"Well, it's enough adventure for *me.* Who's for a swim?"

As soon as the twins' faces brightened, Chips dashed from the inlet, leading the way in a sand-kicking race back to their picnic spot. Though Mandy had to stop and retrieve her canvas bag, Alex caught up with Chips and the two of them shrieked as the chilly water splashed over them.

Once Mandy had joined them, Chips concentrated on keeping her charges happy and wet. In the back of her mind, though, she felt strangely uneasy, and kept glancing back at the dense woods behind them. Endless water fights and dunkings later, the twins fell back on their towels in the sun in a state of happy exhaustion.

Chips stayed in the water long enough to swim a few laps and enjoy the bracing coolness as it soothed her overheated skin—and imagination. It was obvious that this tip of the island and the famous Pilgrim Cove were wonderfully secluded for partying teenagers *and* for mysterious skippers. The fact that the view was obscured by the lighthouse and the overgrown vegetation made her realize how isolated the three of them were at the moment.

Why was the skipper's boat there at all?

Chips stepped out of the water intending to get the nine-year-olds back on their feet and into the boat. As she drew closer to the twins, Chips could see them bent over their treasures. Alex was fingering a handful of shells while Mandy, realizing Chips was coming up behind her, hastily thrust something larger back into her bag.

Chips fell to her knees on the towel. "Okay, Amanda Bailey, if you're trying to sneak a horseshoe crab back into the Lightning, I'll make you walk the plank."

Alex looked from his sister to Chips. "We weren't gonna keep it, honest. Mandy just wanted to look at it."

Chips wrinkled her nose. "If it's dead, it'll smell terrible, and if it's alive, it'll die. So you can't win."

"Chips, don't be angry. I just wanted to look at it. I was gonna put it back, really . . ."

Chips was not even aware of which twin was talking. Her eyes were riveted on the perfect replica of a sea gull that Mandy had sheepishly pulled from the bag with both hands.

"Where did you get that?" Chips demanded.

"I wasn't gonna keep it," Mandy said, fingering the wooden beak.

"You haven't answered me."

Alex punched his sister in the ribs with his elbow. "She got it from the boat. It was tangled up with the lobster pots. I told her to leave it there. Now you've ruined everything," he finished angrily, glaring at his sister.

"I have not."

"Yes, you have. You're so dumb, you can't do anything right."

"Mandy!" Raising her voice nearly an octave made them both hush and look at her.

"I just wanted a closer look. I thought it was a duck like my mother collects, but it's only a dumb sea gull, anyway."

Chips turned the decoy over in her hands, fascinated. It was expertly carved and hand painted. Lifelike, she thought, glancing back at the lighthouse where she knew a second one still sat.

On the bottom was a design, a sort of oval with the initials of the artist, which Chips couldn't make out. She squinted at them, trying to decipher the letters.

The twins were still apologizing profusely as she got to her feet and looked down from one embarrassed face to the other.

"I'm returning this right now. You two stay put until I get back. Pack the hamper, it's time to go."

With the possible exception of going to the Sophomore Dance with Harold Peterson, Chips could not think of anything she'd ever done that she wanted to do *less* than march back along the shore to Pilgrim Cove.

And besides, with Harold, she hadn't felt scared, she had just felt annoyed that he'd asked her two months ahead of time barring all other possibilities. Of course, she convinced herself she wasn't really scared now, just . . . apprehensive.

Like a soldier, Chips forced herself to keep going, concentrating on how nice it would feel to dance with Ryan and how what she really wanted more than anything else in the world was to have him right there, walking with her. Now.

"But he's not here," she whispered out loud, reminding herself that she was in charge of those little nine-year-old pests. She was supposed to be taking care of them, and it was time now to get them off the island.

Her bare toes kicked at the small sand creatures, stones, and shells. The tide was going out, giving her a wider stretch to walk on, but instinctively she hugged the scrubby shoreline—in case someone were watching.

The poor guy was obviously trying to trap lobsters; he had

some sort of system that used decoys, and she had rudely plopped down in the middle of it. *I'd be angry, too,* she thought, pausing at the mouth of the inlet.

The receding tide had reduced the river to a stream, and the mud was glistening in the heat. Taking a deep breath, Chips turned and followed the trickling water into the pines. But after half a dozen steps she stopped, puzzled.

The boat was gone.

She looked again, tiptoeing through the mud and then deeper into the beach plum. Her heart jumped. It wasn't gone. It had been dragged nearly six feet deeper into the undergrowth. Angry indentations in the sand indicated even to her eye that someone had pushed against the stern until it slid from sight. Someone who had been watching them.

4

Chips was leaning over the stern of the boat with the painted sea gull in her outstretched hand when muffled cries made her turn her head. She heard them again. Unmistakable shouts, and without looking back, she threw the decoy into the boat and raced back to the beach.

Chips ran around the bend in sight of the Lightning with her chest heaving. Her bathing-suit straps dug into her shoulders from the effort of gasping for air, and in her overheated imagination she pictured the twins in the clutches of the bearded skipper.

They were in a grip, all right, but not of the skipper. Of the wind. Chips dug her feet into the sand, braking her pace, and watched in amazement as the twins flailed their arms and screamed in unison, not for Chips but at each other—and not from the shore, but from the boat.

Alex had hoisted the sail and was clinging to the halyard as Mandy pushed the tiller, first in one direction, then the other. With each yank of the line, the sail filled, snapping the boom back and forth across the little boat. It was moving.

"The centerboard!" Alex was screaming, frantically trying to weave his line around the cleat. "You forgot to lower the centerboard!"

"Not till we're underway," Mandy was yelling back at him. "Chips never puts it all the way down until we're underway."

The sail seeming finally to have made up its mind, filled the starboard and pulled them into a jibe the moment Alex secured the halyard and pulled in the sheet.

"We are underway, dummy," Alex shot back, nearly hysterical, "and we're going to crash right into Bug Light!"

Had she not been so frightened by the hidden lobster boat and angry with her students' chronic irresponsibility, Chips would have doubled over in laughter. As it was, she waded toward them, cupping her hands around her mouth.

"You're at anchor! Kids." She tried again: "You're still anchored. It's all right." How could two children get into so much trouble!

She waded to the boat, and threw her weight onto the gunwale, clinging to the side. Four terrified eyes finally turned to her. "Let go," she barked, "of everything!"

The moment they obeyed, the sail luffed and the Lightning stopped. "Drop the halyard," she ordered as Alex hastily undid the cleat, letting go of the line holding up the sail. It slid in its metal track down the mast. With a crack, the boom fell to the side deck, narrowly missing Mandy's shoulder, and a heap of nylon looped over Alex and out into the water.

From under the sail, he began to cry, but before Chips uttered another command, they were out of the boat and scurrying to shore. By the time Chips had pulled the sail back into the boat and waded back, Alex's brief tears were gone and both twins had buckled themselves into their orange life vests.

"We were trying to surprise you by rigging the Lightning ourselves."

"We thought you'd be proud of us."

"I guess you're mad at us instead, huh?"

"Are you going to tell Mom about the sea gull?"

Chips was already shaking her head, but she heaved a sigh before she spoke. "I know you meant well. I just wish you'd stop being so independent. No, I don't mean that. I want you to be independent 'cause that's what makes great sailors. That and following directions. Just slow down for a while, both of you, and *listen*."

She smiled at Mandy and mussed up her hair. "I'm going to tell your mother that you're full of curiosity and anxious to learn."

Both twins looked relieved and agreed that it was time to return to the Jimmersons' mooring. The outgoing tide, rushing into open water, made another turn around the lighthouse impossible. While neither twin volunteered to sail, Chips kidded around with them until they regained their self-confidence; and within the hour, both of them were busy tacking back and forth across the channel in the direction of the Jimmerson dock.

As they put Bug Light behind them, the talk of pirates subsided. Once back at their mooring, Chips presented them both with handwritten diplomas and the gift certificates for Nana's. First one, then the other wrapped their arms around Chip's neck.

"This was the most exciting week of my whole life!"

"Maybe we could talk Mom into signing us up for another week in August!"

"I'm all booked up." Chips laughed, trying not to sound too relieved. She knew that another week with the Bailey twins would be enough to make her retire at the tender age of sixteen from her sailing career. They pedaled off arguing about the thrills of sailing versus boardsailing. Chips picked up the empty hamper and headed for the house, noting to herself that there was no sign of the new gardener.

With hours to go until dinner and time on her hands, Chips plopped herself down on the couch in the den and picked up the phone. Marcy McElroy answered on the first ring. "Giving up sailing for soccer?" her friend teased, demanding every detail of the rumor that Chips had been at Nana's with "Mr. Perfection."

Chips obliged happily, enjoying the fluttery feeling she got inside when she talked about Ryan. She told Marcy all about their first evening together and the upcoming sailing lesson. In fact, by the time the conversation was finished, Chips's stomach felt so full of butterflies that she decided to relax with a swim.

Wading out from their beach, she launched into a series of laps, then plopped down, pleasantly exhausted, on her beach towel. She had brought along her cassette player and after pulling on the earphones, she closed her eyes and lost herself in the voice of Tina Turner, which was throbbing in her ears. Thoughts of which bathing suit to wear in the morning were floating through her mind, when all of a sudden she felt a cool hand on her sunburned shoulder. Her eyes flew open in surprise.

She was looking directly into the sun, so for half a second she was blinded. She tried madly to focus as she pulled the pounding music away from her ears.

Ryan stood before her. He was laughing at her startled expression. "I didn't mean to scare you," his lips were mouthing as she put down the earphones.

Chips laughed at herself. She sat up and patted the sand. "Pull up a piece of sand and have a seat. I'm fine. I just didn't hear you because of the music."

He laughed too and sat down, pulling the jersey of his soccer uniform over his head. Chips couldn't help noticing how taut and sculpted the muscles of his chest looked. "Ah, that sea breeze feels soooo cool," he said. "I thought I'd roast out on the field this afternoon. Actually I stopped by on my way home to make sure we're still on for tomorrow. I already told the guys we'd ride over to Outer Beach by boat."

He sat back as though he'd said they'd drop from the sky by helicopter. Chips couldn't help wondering which was more important to him: the time he spent with her or his mode of travel.

"Ryan, I thought you wanted to sail out around the lighthouse. I found the weirdest stuff there today with the Bailey twins. The skipper's boat, the guy who stopped me on the way to Nana's . . . I found it shoved way up in the bushes in Pilgrim Cove. There was a gull decoy in it and another one propped on the ladder of Bug Light. I'd love to show you . . . I just can't get it out of my mind."

Ryan did not hide his annoyance. "Mellow out, Chips, you're probably driving the guy crazy, hauling around a couple of little brats, getting in his way. Come on, there are lots of places to sail without going over there. You're letting your imagination go haywire. It would be a lot more fun at Outer Beach than dodging some furious lobsterman on the island—unless you want to have a private picnic with me in the cove."

Chips studied him carefully to see whether he was serious. She couldn't tell from his voice what he was implying. "What *do* you suppose the guy is doing with his boat in there?"

"Beats me." He shrugged. "I don't know anybody who's been over there much since the town started allowing four-wheel-drive vehicles to use the beach, except for guys looking for a little privacy."

Chips let the final comment drop, not sure how he wanted her to respond. Instead she let her heart race as her eyes rested on the sun-streaked hair. His ruddy Irish coloring was heightened by the freckles on his nose, brought out by hours of soccer in the sun. His eyes looked so blue, bluer than any she had ever seen, she thought.

Chips felt herself practically melting into the sand as he closed his eyes and leaned over, kissing her. They both took a deep breath and smiled at each other, and Ryan helped her to her feet.

"Gotta run," he said simply.

Chips walked with him up the brick path to the house. Next to Ryan's sports car, her father's sedan now sat boxed in on the other side by the all-too-familiar Jeep with the unmistakable red, white, and blue sail wound around the mast and hitched on the roof rack.

Jeffrey Taylor's presence was a cloud on a perfect day, and as he appeared around the corner of the house, Chips stood on tiptoes and kissed Ryan on the cheek. She knew her behavior was immature, but she enjoyed the sense of sophistication it gave her.

As soon as Ryan had gone, she turned on her heels and returned to the beach, annoyed at herself for the twinge of foolishness she felt because of her behavior.

Back on her beach towel, earphones in place, she tried to concentrate on Tina Turner again. Then she felt the vibrations of running footsteps on the lawn behind her.

Chips sat up and opened her eyes, but as she tried to look behind her, she caught only a blur of motion. She had just enough time to duck down as the fully clothed form of Jeff Taylor bounded cleanly over her head and shoulders and into the water beyond.

When Chips lifted her face up from where she had buried it in her hands, she saw nothing in front of her but mad splashing and kicking, which eventually settled into long even strokes. As the gardener/caretaker came up for air, he gave her a big wave and disappeared into the water. She did not return his wave.

In spite of herself, Chips watched, surprised to feel those butterflies again. She took off the earphones and waited. No Jeff.

Soon the butterflies turned to a knot of tension, though, as Chips leaped to her feet. Her eyes were riveted on the spot where he had last surfaced. Nothing.

The tension turned to a jolt of alarm. "Jeff!" she called once. Then she stood up, counted to ten, and raced to the edge of the water.

"Jeff!" She repeated as the water hit her knees, slowing her stride.

Then, without warning, less than five feet from where she stood, Jeff's head popped out of the water. He stood up with both arms raised, hands curved like claws on either side of him.

"Dracula lives!" he trumpeted, as the water fell off him in sheets.

Chips gasped and tried to sputter indignantly. Then she lost her balance and fell backward into an undignified sitting position, the water lapping around her waist.

"Dracula," jeans and polo shirt clinging to him, plopped down next to her, watching with amusement as she tried not to smile.

"You scared the life out of me, Jeff Taylor. I thought you'd drowned."

"Would you have cared?"

"No. But my father doesn't like bodies cluttering up the beach."

He laughed, shaking water from his hair while Chips tried not to pay attention to the fact that the fluttering in her stomach was back.

"Couldn't stand it another minute," Jeff was explaining, still sitting in the water.

"What?"

"The heat. Your mother gave me a list as long as my arm of stuff to do, but I'm through for today. Too darn hot."

This time Chips looked at him thoughtfully, grudgingly admiring the even temperament that seemed always to make him so much at ease. "Why do you work so hard?"

"Partly because I have to, partly because I want to. I want to be a landscape architect, and gardening—that is, setting right something like your old flower beds—is a challenge. It doesn't seem that much like work."

"Unless it's ninety degrees out," Chips threw in, making him laugh.

"Unless it's ninety," he repeated. "My folks have gone out on a limb to pay for my education, so there's not much left over for extras."

"Like sailboards?"

He nodded. "And lift tickets in the winter."

It was the perfect opportunity to ask about his school and where he went skiing, but Chips found herself battling a sudden case of shyness. The feeling washed over her and she couldn't think of a thing to say without making it seem like she was too interested in his private life. So she just nodded and pulled herself out of the salt water.

After she scooped up the tape player and towel, they walked together along the brick path to the house. The slosh, slosh, slosh of Jeff's jeans rubbing together finally made Chips giggle. When they reached the back door, she looked up at him.

"I didn't mean to scare you, Chips," he said quietly.

She shrugged her shoulders. "That's all right, Jeff, but one more second and I would have dragged you out by your chin."

He smiled again. "Gee, I'm sorry I didn't hold my breath that extra second."

Before she had time to figure out why his answer had given her such a happy feeling, Jeff was shaking out his hair and moving toward his jeep.

"You ski, sailor?" he asked, opening the door.

"You bet," came easily from Chips. She watched as he looked at the spot where Ryan's car had been.

"Soccer captain ski, too?"

"I don't know," she answered hotly, a sudden wash of embarrassment making her blush as she thought about how dumb she must have looked to him kissing Ryan before.

She went into the house, angry and confused about how she felt so awkward when Jeffrey Taylor was around.

*　　*　　*

"I don't like the sound of it," Paul Jimmerson said, putting down his fork. Chips and her parents were eating dinner on the screened porch, and halfway through her story of the day's adventures, her father's face had clouded.

To Chips's consternation, however, it was not in sympathy for her "overheated imagination," as he put it, but for the skipper.

"Chips," he finished less roughly, "the fellow has a right to be concerned about a teenager and two children sailing around his lobster pots. He has no idea whether you're a capable sailor or not, and from what you've told me about the antics of the Baileys, can you blame the guy for being hard on you?"

Her mother put a hand on her daughter's arm. "Frankly, you're lucky you didn't actually run into him on the island—it sounds as though he expected that the words he had with you that night you walked to Nana's would be enough. I don't know a thing about lobstering, but the decoys are obviously some sort of signal. Perhaps he has a fleet of boats, Chips. It's a difficult enough way to earn a living without worrying that every time the tide is high some young sailor is going to foul the lines. The channel is certainly long and wide enough for you and your students without going around the lighthouse."

Chips's heart sank as she finished the last of her potato salad, but she didn't argue because she was afraid that any further discussion might make them actually prohibit her from going out that far. She let the subject drop.

It dropped however to less pleasant news. "The Gordons' house was robbed," her mother spoke up, sending a chill through all of them. "I saw Jake this morning. They were away for three days and came back to find Marcia's dressing room cleaned out."

"Mrs. Gordon always did wear too much jewelry," Chips blurted out, immediately regretting her poor joke as both parents glared at her.

"Hiring Jeff Taylor was an excllent idea, Paul. And Chips, I shouldn't have to tell you that this is not humorous, not humorous in the least. I will certainly feel safer while we're in Denver knowing Jeff is helping keep this property occupied."

Dr. Jimmerson nodded and looked at Chips. "Now, let's find something to talk about that will cheer us all up."

"Ryan Kennedy and I are going sailing tomorrow," she sighed.

"Best news I've heard all day." Her father laughed, reaching across the table playfully to muss his daughter's hair.

*   *   *

Although not a knowledgeable sailor, Ryan Kennedy was completely familiar with the harbor—in addition to being a natural athlete. The same skill he applied to soccer, water skiing, even tennis, he brought to the Lightning.

After dutifully shaking hands with her parents and commenting on the fine weather, he walked Chips across the lawn to the dock. She smiled under his appreciative glance, glad she'd taken the time to choose (after trying on three different outfits) her most flattering bathing suit—a red and white maillot with horizontal stripes, wide at the top and narrow across the hips. She hoped it gave the illusion of a little more above, a little less below. Ryan had on a blue (oh, how it matched his eyes!) polo shirt and navy trunks, and both sailors wore rubber-soled boat shoes.

Ryan took the oars to the dinghy, and Chips sat in the stern. "This would be a good time to serenade me," she said, trying to sound serious.

"You've got to be kidding!"

Chips shrugged. "It's the least you can do if I teach you to sail." While she rigged the boat he burst into an off-key rendition of a Michael Jackson song. The sail flapped madly as Chips clasped her hands over her ears. "Forget I mentioned it," she shouted, laughing.

He grabbed her wrists and with a gentle tug brought Chips down next to him on the seat. She was just about to tell him to lean over the bow and undo the line that held them to the mooring. But first things first, she said to herself, as they drew close to each other. He pressed his lips warmly against hers. Like sunshine itself, Chips thought, sighing contentedly, kissing him back.

When they finally got around to freeing the boat, the Lightning skimmed out under the steady wind. Chips guided the tiller while Ryan held the sheet, the line controlling the sail. All the while they snuggled comfortably next to each other.

They took a wide tack across the basin in the direction of the lighthouse. "Boy, you sure learn quicker than the Bailey twins!"

Ryan smiled and looked up into the sail. "By the time we hit Outer Beach, I want to look like I'm a pro." He gave her another smile. "I sure have found the right teacher."

Flip, flop went her stomach. Chips felt flushed with a mixture of happiness and excitement. She chose her words carefully. "Then let's take the time to go by way of Bug Light. It'll take longer, I know, but then you can practice *and* I'll get a chance to show you where that decoy was perched."

Ryan frowned. "Hey, look, Chips, I don't want to go chasing after some dumb mysterious stranger."

"We won't. I just want to see if the decoy's still up on the lighthouse steps. It's some kind of signal, I'm sure . . . from the guy who stopped me the other night. I want you to see for yourself."

Ryan sighed and nodded reluctantly as they caught a gust of wind and tightened the sail. Chips wished he wouldn't act quite so impatient with her. They zigzagged across the choppy water, getting closer to the mouth of the harbor with every tack until finally Bug Light was sharply in focus.

But the current was stronger than last time, and the trip seemed to take forever. To pass the time, Chips entertained Ryan with stories of the Baileys as she instructed him on how to handle the boat. By the time they were ready to approach the Bug, Ryan was at the helm and Chips's adrenaline was making her pulse race. If the decoy was still there, she would like nothing better than to scramble up the ladder after it and hand him the proof.

Proof of what, she thought to herself, recalling the discussion with her parents. Proof that someone is trying to make a living from lobstering? Proof that the evil-looking skipper is signaling somebody? Proof, most likely, that Chips Jimmerson has an overactive imagination.

"I'd better take the tiller here," she said out loud to Ryan. "The shoals can be tricky, even with the water high."

Gulls were already shrieking in protest as the iron-plated column loomed ahead, and Chips brought her hand up to shield her eyes. She looked up first at the circling birds as they caught the breeze, diving and shrieking in anger at the intrusion.

With a start, she remembered to scan the water for lobster pot bobbers, sheepishly recalling the warning from her parents for the second time. To her relief there were none within striking range, only a red and white marker far off to starboard.

The Lightning was skimming silently into the shadow of the lighthouse. Ryan grew quiet, also holding his hand up against the glare as he scanned the landmark.

Above them the iron structure seemed enormous, dwarfing the little boat and its occupants. Chips's view was momentarily blocked by Ryan's back, but when he shook his head she knew without looking that the ladder was empty.

"There's nothing up there," he said, sounding annoyed, as though she couldn't now see perfectly well for herself.

"It was there yesterday, Ryan. I sailed the twins right here—twice, in fact, just to be sure." She pointed to the empty rung as the boat skimmed past, headed for the island.

"From what you told me, maybe those squirmy students of yours distracted you. Look, we're practically out of range already and we're both paying attention. How could you ever have had time to make sure there was a decoy up there with two obnoxious nine-year-olds climbing all over the boat? It doesn't make any sense, anyway." Ryan looked at Chips with a mixture of impatience and sympathy.

The gulls were already returning to the lighthouse, and at least half a dozen of them perched on the rungs of the ladder. "That's probably what you saw, and we've spent a couple of hours just getting here. Since we've come this far, how about a private picnic . . . just us . . . in the cove?"

Chips looked into his face, thinking of his kisses. His fingers tightened over hers, pulling her hand back from where she'd been pointing at the ladder, but the sound of an outboard motor erased anything either of them was about to say. The sudden wake from the oncoming boat slapped angrily against the Lightning, making it rock precariously.

"Head into the wind," she ordered tensely, since Ryan's hand was still on the tiller. Keeping her left hand wound in his, she let the sheet slacken in her right until the boat was bobbing at a standstill.

It was her second close look at the face, though this time the stubble had thickened into a beard and his eyes were hidden behind dark glasses. He spoke to Ryan as though Chips were invisible.

"Keep your girl friend away from the light," he yelled over the idling engine. "Tell her to stay back in the basin with them fool kids. Somebody's gonna get hurt out here in open water!"

"You're right, I've been trying to tell her that all morning," Ryan shot back, nodding in complete agreement.

Chips felt her face glow, hotter than the July sun could have made it. Yanking her fingers from Ryan's grasp, she leaned over and looked into the twin reflections of the black lenses. "I know what I'm doing. I'm certified by the Coast Guard and the Red Cross." She tried not to sound belligerent, but it was impossible to lower her voice to be heard over the engine. She waved her hand lightly, in order to appear friendly.

"Please don't worry about your lobster pots, I've been sailing for years. I'm qualified, really. You can check with the harbor master."

It was obvious to Chips that something she had said made him stiffen, his jaw muscles working in anger, and she wished she could see his eyes. But even the thin line of his mouth made her shiver and feel creepy.

Without giving Ryan an explanation, Chips took the tiller from him and yanked in the sheet. They caught the wind and were underway as a curse from the skipper caught the breeze and floated after them.

The outboard motor churned the waters again and he flew in the opposite direction, out into Plymouth Bay behind the lighthouse.

"Thanks a lot for backing me up," were Chips's first sour words.

"I agree with him."

"Well, did you see his face the minute I mentioned his pots? He was furious. I'll bet he's a poacher, probably stealing from legitimate traps and selling them himself. That's why he hasn't got a decent boat and he hides in the cove!"

"Why can't you just believe him? He thinks you and your

boatful of kids will be out here snooping around all summer, fouling all his pots." Ryan's voice was filled with exasperation, Chips's with anger, and the only problem with arguing in the boat was that there was no place to go.

Shoulder to shoulder they sat, fuming at each other, getting closer to Outer Beach. "Prepare to come about," Chips finally said, pulling in the sheet.

"Hardly," Ryan answered, shoving the tiller to change tacks.

"Hardly?" Despite the tension in the air, Chips began to laugh.

"Hardly. Isn't that what I'm supposed to say when we turn?"

"Hard a lee," she corrected, finally unable to suppress a chuckle any longer. "It means push the tiller hard to the leeward side."

Chips watched Ryan's face anxiously for a sign that she'd made him angrier, but he burst into a smile at his mistake and calmly replied "hardly," for the rest of the tacks to the beach.

Unfortunately the tide was well on its way out by the time they beached the boat, and Chips could tell at a glance that most of the kids Ryan had expected had already left. The beach was nearly deserted.

With the water low and the centerboard up, all they had to do to beach the Lightning was drag it up a few yards onto the sand. Ryan was unpleasantly silent while they busied themselves with the task and then carried the picnic hamper and towels to the small band of teenagers who were still lying in the sun.

Chips recognized the faces from Nana's, and all the kids greeted her cheerfully. "Hey, Ryan," one of the boys said, "tide's going out. We're just about to leave. Everybody else left a half-hour ago."

As she pretended to busy herself with the food, Chips heard Ryan's terse reply:

"We would have been here this morning, but Nancy Drew had to sail us on a wild goose chase around the lighthouse."

5

The kids who were left stayed long enough to devour the bag of pretzels Chips had packed for lunch and to make plans for the upcoming week. Most of them had some kind of summer job, but it sounded to Chips as though every clear evening there was an endless round of beach parties.

She smiled at the thought of Outer Beach by moonlight, bonfires, and Ryan's undivided attention. Maybe she really should cool her "overactive imagination," stop worrying about the skipper, and concentrate on the soccer captain instead.

While she sat there daydreaming, Ryan got up to help load the Land Rover parked at the edge of the sandy trail. When she realized that he expected her to wave good-bye to the departing group, she scrambled up next to him feeling thrilled to have his arm around her shoulder.

They waved a final time and moved quickly back to the towels to avoid the dust being kicked up by the vehicle as it bit into the sand and headed for the parking lot at the town end of the beach.

"Nancy Drew?" Chips said as they reached for the sandwiches.

Ryan shrugged. "Teenage detective on a wild goose chase."

"Maybe, but you do have to admit it was a great sail."

"Yeah, I hard-a-lee-a-gree!"

Chips groaned and laughed and put the skipper out of her mind. She wanted to enjoy the undivided attention of her date. The return trip, after their meal and a walk along the beach hand-in-hand, was more direct and trouble free.

After walking the boat to the deep water, Ryan offered to sail the entire way back. Chips was secretly impressed with how fast he learned. Rarely did she have to repeat an instruction and, unlike many boys she knew, he was happy to be corrected so that he could get things right. Of course, Chips thought, that's what makes him the captain of the team—a strong athlete who follows directions from the coach.

"There's a lobster pot off to port," Chips said moments later while he headed away.

"Aye, aye, Captain, no more angry skippers," he shot back with a smile.

By the time they returned to the dock and stowed the gear, the smell of steak over charcoal filled the air. Dr. Jimmerson was standing over the grill outside the porch as they came up the steps, and he insisted that Ryan stay for dinner.

Over the meal, Ryan was relaxed and animated in the company of the Jimmersons, and Chips could tell by her parents' lively conversation that they liked him. Ryan touched briefly on the fact that they'd been out around the lighthouse, adding that they hadn't seen a thing.

Dr. Jimmerson immediately gave his daughter an "I hope you're using your good judgment" look, which she countered with her brightest smile. "Trust me," she hoped it said.

The feeling of wanting to be left alone with a boy—not any boy, *Ryan*—was a new one for Chips. She kind of felt surprised by it as she patiently helped clear the table. Compared with Ryan, Harold Peterson and the handful of other boys she'd dated last year seemed like such jerks. She remembered that with them she had positively welcomed double-dating, crowded dance floors, and well-lighted driveways.

Her father entertained Ryan with the family story about Chips running the Lightning aground with her grandmother aboard, right in front of all the other old ladies on the porch of the Yacht Club. As he rambled on, she gazed longingly from the kitchen into the dusky summer night and back to the soccer captain.

When she returned to the table, she found an excuse to grab his arm. "Don't you dare listen to Dad," she cried. "He's ruining my image!"

But within a few minutes, she realized that her parents weren't ruining anything. In fact, Chips suddenly realized, they were treating her as maturely as they did Melissa. Dr. Jimmerson excused himself, explaining that he had a lot of paperwork to do, and her mother actually flicked on the floodlight that il-luminated the boathouse and beach.

"Fresh towels are in the laundry room in case you two want one last swim," she was saying, moving from the kitchen.

Within minutes, Chips and Ryan were walking the path from the house back to the water, silent until they stood barefoot in the sand. Out ahead of them the small flash from the lighthouse broke into fragments on the water. It was a scene she'd seen every night of her life, but not until this moment had it seemed even remotely romantic.

"Tide's coming in," Ryan said softly.

"Mmmm," she replied. "Thanks for not mentioning running into the skipper."

Though it was dark, in the shadows cast by the floodlight on the boathouse, she could see Ryan turn to face her. His fingers touched her bare shoulder, and she was aware of how warm his touch was.

Chips knew she was being compared to Mary Thompson, the senior he had dated, who seemed to be perfectly happy just basking in Ryan's glow from the Harvest Dance right through to her Senior Prom. In fact, Chips couldn't think of much that made Mary stand out except that she had been Ryan's girl all last year.

As if they were in a crowd, Ryan put his mouth next to her ear. "I just wish you'd slow down long enough for me to teach *you* some things. It's only fair, you know, after my all-day sailing lesson."

Before she could think of a reply, he kissed her, both warm hands sliding around her shoulders. A breeze picked up the hair on the back of her neck, and she shivered.

Ryan laughed softly. "You can kiss me back, just drop the beach towels."

Chips laughed, too, letting the terry cloth fall on their feet as she returned the kiss. Chips suddenly felt a little breathless and pulled away.

She was relieved that Ryan sensed her reluctance and dropped down on the towels, spreading them together to make room for both of them. No sooner had they sat down, than Ryan began, "If the weather stays this hot, there'll be a beach party tomorrow night. What do you say?" Ryan asked, his voice husky.

"To going with you?"

He stared at her. "Of course to going with me!"

Chips smiled at him. "I'd love to."

All of a sudden, Chips was on her feet, dashing for the water.

"No fair," she heard him yell from behind her as he pulled his polo shirt over his head.

The chill of the inky water shocked her skin, as she plunged in, making her whoop as she came up for air. No sooner had she filled her lungs than she felt his hands around her waist. He lifted her up out of the sea, and dunked her back in.

"No fair," she coughed and laughed and sputtered. "I can't lift you up."

"I thought you could do anything," Ryan teased, and Chips turned to him before bending her knees and disappearing back under the water. With all her weight, she sprang from the bottom, high enough to pounce with both hands on his shoulders. This time he went over in a good solid dunking and came up spurting salt water. For a moment she thought she was in for more of the same, but his hands were on her shoulders for balance. His face caught the light as a salty kiss brushed her lips.

They walked out of the water holding hands until her teeth began to chatter with the chill of the night air on her wet skin. "Grab your towel," she said, "and I'll race you to the house."

When they finally said good-night, Ryan's hair was still wet, his handsome face bright from a day in the sun. "I learned a lot today, Nancy Drew," he joked, getting into the car.

She wrinkled her nose, then grinned. "Next time, no detective work."

"There'd better not be," Ryan quipped, and the smile faded from Chips's face.

She stood outside long enough to watch the tail lights until they were two tiny red dots at the head of the lane. She turned around, peered at the flashing lighthouse for another minute, and then went up to her room.

* * *

It was hot at the beginning of the Jimmersons' last week in Snug Harbor together. This kind of heat was rare for the town, and the only relief was on the water. The village shimmered as the heat seemed to rise in waves from the streets, the beaches were crowded, and even before Chips prepared for her morning class, the bay was dotted with sails.

Before meeting her new students, Chips took her bike into town on an errand, her bright yellow T-shirt already clinging to her skin by the time she reached the post office. She felt sticky and irritated that just to buy one air-mail stamp for France she had to stand behind three people. Wishing the little post office were air conditioned, she tried to concentrate on the fact that Ryan had called before he left for camp to confirm their date for the beach party tomorrow night.

The woman in front of Chips fumbled with three packages. Worse than the Christmas rush, Chips thought, wiping her wrist across her sweaty forehead.

Her hand froze above her eyes as a hand, twice the size of hers, seized her shoulder. She began to turn around, but the grip tightened painfully. The deep voice, barely audible even to Chips, was right in her ear.

"No need to turn, just listen."

The skipper! Her blood pounded so loudly in her ears she had trouble hearing him, but the tone of his voice was unmistakable.

"If you don't mind your own business, I'm going to take you to the harbor master myself. Quit nosing around where you don't belong, kid. Got it?"

Still stunned, Chips didn't move. The fingers tightened again.

"I'm asking you if you understand."

She nodded, staring into the back of the woman in front of her. The fingers loosened, and she felt herself being propelled around. She blinked at the bearded face with its dark glasses and tight-lipped mouth. No one seemed to notice that anything was amiss, and she realized with a shudder that he had been smiling pleasantly the entire time. "Atta girl," he added, giving her a bright smile. And while she stood speechless, he turned on his heel and left the post office.

"May I help you?"

Chips turned back and with shaking fingers pushed her coins across the counter.

*　　*　　*

Though her only advertising was word of mouth and a small card tacked on the bulletin board at the town landing, Chips's classes were booked solidly. Most of the children, like the Bailey twins, were either year-round residents or regular visitors returning every summer.

Chips rode her bike back to the house, trying to think about the two friendly little faces who would be waiting to greet her, rather than the sinister one she'd just seen.

"Harbor master, sure," she muttered. Whatever it was the skipper was up to, she had a hard time imagining that he'd want Mr. Ransom to know anything about it.

As Chips braked her bicycle in her driveway, two of the most precocious twelve-year olds she'd ever seen slid out of the back of an oversized black sedan, waving the chauffeur off before Chips had a chance to introduce herself to him.

No ten-speed bikes for these two! Considering the heat, Chips had expected them to arrive in bathing suits. (She was in her navy blue tank suit and her scuffed Topsiders.) What she did not expect was matching string bikinis, one pink with white dots, the other white with pink dots . . . and matching nail polish.

Chips looked from the enameled fingers to the chic New York haircuts and finally down to spotless brown leather Topsiders, so new the rawhide laces couldn't be tied tightly. She had half expected spike heels.

"Well," she began cheerfully," I'm Chips Jimmerson. You must be the cousins from Manhattan."

They nodded. "Lauren Delveccio," said the dark-haired girl. "Amy Delveccio," said the blonde. Chips ushered them out to the dock wondering to herself why anyone would wear green eyeshadow to a sailing lesson.

The first crisis hit before they even left land. "You don't *honestly* expect us to wear these totally gross life jackets!"

Chips smiled. "For sure. Unless you can swim from here to the Lightning and back."

Amy looked at Lauren. "No one said anything about *getting wet!*"

Lauren looked at Amy. "They're orange."

Chips looked at both of them. "International orange, a color that might save your life if you ever capsize."

They just looked at her with their green-lidded eyes. "I know, I know. 'No one said anything about getting wet.' "

The lesson progressed at a snail's pace, with both girls clinging to the sides for dear life the minute the Lightning heeled the least little bit. Try as she might to explain that tilting made the boat sail more efficiently and as long as their weight was evenly distributed no one would fall overboard, Chips could not get them to relax.

Before they'd been on the water an hour, she knew the week would be spent in the gentle confines of the basin, in sight of the landing, the shore, and the harbor master. It was going to take a lot more than certificates to Nana's to bribe these two into enthusiasm.

Chips took the tiller. "We'll go out around the buoy."

Lauren's face brightened. "That boy's awesome," she replied looking over the instructor's shoulder.

As Chips tried to explain that she was talking about the channel marker, not the opposite sex, she heard the sound of her name drifting from the direction in which both girls were now staring.

"Chips, ahoy!" Jeff Taylor skimmed past the Lightning, expertly maneuvering his board by shifting his weight. "She's a great teacher," he was calling. "Pay attention, and you'll be the best sailors in the bay."

The tanned, brown-haired boardsailor pulled up alongside, stole their wind, and shot past after flashing Chips his fabulous grin.

Lauren suddenly decided that she wanted to try holding the tiller; Amy asked to handle the lines. Chips asked silently only to be left alone; it hardly seemed fair that after knocking herself out to produce even a smile from these two, one glance from Jeff and a well-placed comment had them acting as though they were in the Olympic trials.

For the rest of the lesson, the Delveccio cousins worked so diligently and hung so far over the side for better views of the distant sailboard, Chips was glad they were in life jackets. Her fear was not so much of their capsizing, but of falling out of the tops of their string bikinis.

The three of them worked up an honest sweat, which was made worse once the lesson was over because there was no seabreeze. As they hung up the offending life vests, Chips asked if they'd like to take a swim.

It was the first spontaneous behavior she'd seen them exhibit all afternoon, splashing and dunking just as she had the night before with Ryan. Still dripping, Chips dropped onto the sand, closing her eyes. Behind her the shrieking and carrying on reminded her far more of the nine-year-old twins than of girls old enough to think an eighteen-year-old was "awesome."

She drifted into daydreams about her own awesome date with Ryan until, with a start, Chips realized that the shouting and laughing had stopped.

A sliver of fear shot through her as she opened her eyes and sat up, looking hard and fast back at the water. It was a relief to see that Lauren and Amy were fine, standing knee deep and painfully dignified. Their posture told Chips immediately what had caused the change, and she whirled around as Jeffrey Taylor dropped neatly down beside her.

She was totally unprepared for the thrill of excitement she felt to have him sitting so close to her, but passed it off as some kind of effect her silly students were having on her.

"Reluctant students, I guess," he said for openers, making her knit her brow. "You stayed in the basin, close to home. No Clark's Island and peeking from the bluff for these girls."

Chips's stomach tightened into an angry knot. She was surprised. He had seen them on Friday! Once again she felt flustered in front of him, though Jeff was acting oblivious of the sudden blush that had suffused her cheeks. *Why hadn't he said something, if he'd been on the island, too? Had he been hiding from them for some strange reason?*

"What were you doing there?"

The brown eyes looked into hers. "Exploring. Just like you."

Just like me? Had he seen her come across the skipper's boat? Had Jeff been the one who pulled it back into the brush? *No,* she reminded herself. They had watched him sail off toward Outer Beach. At least until they left the bluff . . .

"I haven't got much free time left," he was saying, "before your folks leave for Denver. I've already started clearing the perennial beds in front of the house."

Ugh. The reference to Jeff's upcoming employment stung like a thorn, and she looked up as the girls strolled over sedately. Jeff got to his feet and held out his hand for Chips, who let him help her up, surprised at how warm his fingers were.

"Girls, I'd like you to meet Jeff Taylor, the sailboarder you were admiring this morning. Jeff, these are my students, Lauren and Amy Delveccio."

The twelve-year-olds extended their hands gracefully in his direction, and Jeff shook them, giving the girls his famous grin.

"You must be one of the best sailboarders on the bay," Lauren said, suddenly demure.

He shook his head. "Your captain's the best on the bay."

He smiled at Chips, but she still couldn't tell whether he was kidding her or not. Before she could make up her mind, he excused himself and raced to the water, diving in cleanly. "Oh, truly excellent," Lauren whispered.

While Jeff was still swimming, the limousine arrived and they turned to leave—but not before assuring Chips that they'd had a wonderful day and couldn't wait until tomorrow. Chips went up for her shower, shaking her head.

By the time she bathed, dried her hair, and got dressed the sun had gone under a cloud but the temperature was as high as ever. She put on mascara and lipstick, hoping they wouldn't run, then looked at herself in the mirror. The boat-neck cotton shirt over simple green shorts should be fine, she told herself, wincing at how curly her hair had gotten in the humid weather.

She went down the front stairs, walked through the dining room to the kitchen, and shouted over the sound of running water. "What's for dinner, Mrs. Porter, I'm starved?"

The water stopped, and so did Chips. Mrs. Porter was not at the sink, Jeff was. He was drying his hands with paper towels but letting the water he had thrown onto his face and shoulders drip onto his chest in cooling rivulets. "Mrs. Porter's gone."

"I can see that."

"She wanted you to know that there's chicken salad in the fridge and the soccer captain will pick you up at seven."

Chips opened the refrigerator. "He has a name, you know."

Jeff's wet hair moved as he nodded. "Ryan Kennedy. I think I caught a glimpse of him being kissed yesterday."

Chips wished that she were a million miles away. Was she always going to feel rude, embarrassed, or immature when Jeff was around? Maybe if they ended up having their meals together while he was house-sitting she would be more herself. Just the thought of spending even a little time with him made her stomach flutter. She frowned.

"Problem?" Those brown eyes were serious for once.

Chips shook her head. "No. Am I supposed to offer you dinner?"

"Not tonight. I've got a date myself. One of my neighbors is anxious to show me some of Snug Harbor's popular spots. Who knows, maybe I'll see you at the beach."

Her frown made him lift her chin as he passed her on the way out the door. "Cheer up. There's enough sand for all of us."

Chips munched her chicken in silence on the porch, annoyed that her thoughts kept returning to the touch of his fingers on her chin. He said a neighbor wanted to show him around town. That confirmed her suspicions that he was new in Snug Harbor. He had mentioned his parents' paying for education, would he be going off to college in the fall? Until this morning, all her objections to him had centered on her desire for independence.

Now two of her students—in bikinis, no less—were absolutely moonstruck over him and some neighbor was dying to take him out. He dates.

Of course he dates, she repeated to herself. *Jeff's eighteen, and if he wants to join the beach party that's none of my business.* She found it frustrating that in a few short days everything she did would end up being his business, while she knew next to nothing about *his.*

"Not that I would ever give him the satisfaction of asking!"

Beach party. Time to think about that! Chips packed an old gray army blanket feeling her heart skip as she thought about how soon she and Ryan would be sitting together on it. Marshmallows? There would probably be a fire. She pulled them off the pantry shelf. A six-pack of soda and a heavy sweater topped off the canvas bag. To Chips, beach parties had always been a little like proms. They sounded romantic and exciting, but inevitably she found herself shivering in the dark with someone like Harold or even worse, a bunch of her girl friends. *Tonight will be different!*

By seven o'clock Dr. and Mrs. Jimmerson were home, and when Ryan arrived he came in for a few minutes of small talk. He promised reluctantly to have Chips home "at a decent hour," and then they left for the party.

The beach parking lot closed at eleven—an automatic breaking point for the summer partying Chips was used to, but Ryan made it clear as they drove out that his crowd usually found another spot so they could stay out later. It was not the first time she felt uneasy with his breezy style, but the thrill of sitting next to him as they headed down Bay Road made her put those feelings out of her mind.

Once in the parking lot, Ryan automatically steered to the far end where a handful of Jeeps and the Land Rover sat. "Hey, look. It's Nancy Drew," one of the kids yelled. Chips took the kidding good-naturedly. She and Ryan climbed into the back of a Jeep, and they all drove down the sandy trail to the tip of the beach.

A bonfire was burning on the rocky shore, tended by a half a dozen of Ryan's friends. Chips was relieved to see that Jeff was not among them, but troubled to see that so many were drinking beer. It was definitely an older and wilder crowd. The group was made up of soon-to-be seniors, those who had just graduated, and a few college kids who were between semesters. Though she was the youngest, all the girls were dressed casually as she was, in shorts or jeans.

She and Ryan busied themselves with spreading the blanket. Gina Crosby, who was also in her French class, put a cassette in her tape player and urged the kids around her to start dancing. One glance around the fire, however, told Chips that the couples were far more interested in staying on their blankets. Poor Gina seemed to be the only one less than crazy about her date—or the drinking.

Ryan offered her a rum and coke. It was the first time Chips was put in a position of having to refuse a drink with Ryan. She didn't want to ruin the party, but she didn't want any liquor. Gina had said "no" and so did she.

As the sun set to the west, then slid behind the trees on the far shore, Ryan held her hand, and they listened to Gina's tape of Huey Lewis. Between the fire and Ryan's arm around her, Chips had no need for a sweater. It seemed a good time to bring up her frightening warning at the post office, but, once again, she discovered Ryan was totally unsympathetic and, she had to admit, uninterested.

The couples sticking to rum and coke became increasingly boisterous so any serious moments with Ryan became impossible. Chips felt as though an invisible wall had sprung up between them, making her feel frustrated and unsure about what to say or do.

Just beyond the group the sand rose in dunes that were topped with slender green eel grass. Couples were wandering off and disappearing over the dunes. She was secretly relieved that, even though Ryan didn't want to talk about the skipper, he was content to sit with her on the blanket. Her contentment died, however, when someone drunkenly offered her another drink.

"Our private beach party last night was more fun," Chips said finally. "Ryan, your friends are a real turn-off sometimes."

She got to her feet, tugged him through the dancers, then raced ahead of him past the dunes and out toward the tip of the sandy spit of land. She was the sailor but he was the soccer star, and it took less than a minute before he caught up. He picked her up and swung her around in the air.

"Don't let them ruin the evening for us, Chips," he said.

She fell panting against his chest. "I don't want to," she replied defensively. His clear blue eyes shone as he looked at her in the dusky light.

Ryan kissed Chips, and for a moment it felt totally wonderful . . . the breathless racing of her heart, his warm arms around her, pulling her in . . .

"Chips," he repeated, "I thought this was going to be one boring summer, all on my own. You sure do liven things up."

"All on my own" . . . She knew he was talking about Mary Thompson, who was away and getting ready for college. How could he bring her up now? Was he still thinking about her even when they were together like this? Chips turned away from his hug and looked over at the dark form of Clark's Island. From Outer Beach's tip it was only a short swim away, though now it was barely visible as the dark settled in.

"Pilgrim Cove is right across the water, isn't it?" she asked, still snuggled into his hug.

It was too dark to see whether he was nodding in agreement, but his fingers tightened over hers before he answered. "If you promise you won't tell any more pirate stories tonight, I'll go over there with you one of these days."

"To explore *the island?*"

Ryan laughed. "You just said you wouldn't run away."

When he turned and gave her a kiss, she returned it with a sigh of contentment. They stood together on the rocky shore, gazing out at the dark water, the only light the stars and the distant fire. Even Bug Light's steady blinking was hidden by the bluff of the island where she'd watched Jeff. How perfect the cove was for clandestine meetings, Chips thought. No one, except partying kids, ever came out this far.

Somewhere to the left of them, a female voice began to giggle. "Oh, I'd be afraid to try it," she was saying. Chips wrinkled her nose at the flirtatious tone. "I'd never get the sail out of the water. Just imagine *me* in a wet suit!"

Far off in the distance, thunder rumbled. "Weather's changing, rain tomorrow," Ryan said with authority. "What do you do with your kids if it rains?"

"Practice knots on the porch and points of sail on paper."

"We do the same thing in the camp rec hall. Strategy and plays on paper." Ryan talked about soccer as they walked and kissed their way back to the fire.

Ten minutes later, as Chips was feeding Ryan marshmallows from the pointed stick in her hand, a dark figure stepped from the shadows into the glow of the embers. She immediately recognized the giggly voice from the dunes. It was Kristen Satterfield, Homecoming Queen and Mary Thompson's best friend.

She was another painful reminder of Mary. But Chips didn't have any time to brood about it. Kristen greeted everyone happily, and if she had been surprised to see who Ryan's date was, she had the good taste to keep it to herself.

Kristen stood in the firelight with her shoulder-length hair blowing softly around her shoulders. Unlike every other girl there, she was in a sundress with row upon row of tiny tucks and buttons on it. A vision, Chips thought glumly, unable to overlook her perfect figure. Kristen had been right. It *was* hard to imagine her in a wet suit.

Chips yanked the last two sugary blobs off her stick and stuck them in her mouth as Kristen turned back to the shadows. "Everybody," she said beaming, "I want you to meet a new friend of mine—in fact, my next door neighbor whose been hiding away in boarding school all year. This is Jeff Taylor."

The gooey glue of the marshmallow stuffed into her mouth was the only thing that kept Chips's lower jaw from dropping to her chest. One minute there was an empty space between Kristen and Ryan—the next, there stood Jeff looking ruggedly handsome in his red and white rugby shirt, jeans, and Docksiders.

He gave everyone a handshake and the famous smile, repeating names, explaining that his family had moved to town last fall from Connecticut. Chips felt her heart pounding. Jeff was so poised in front of all these kids he didn't even know.

The girls around the fire were looking at him the way the boys had looked at Kristen. Ryan was knitting his brow as though trying to place a face that looked familiar.

Chips was not about to tell him that Jeff Taylor was the guy he had seen coming out of her kitchen that day when she had suddenly thrown her arms around him.

". . . soccer captain," Jeff was saying to Ryan. "I hear you've got a tough team."

Ryan was perking up. "Do you play?"

To Chips's utter amazement, Jeff was nodding. "I'm in boarding school just north of Boston. I played center on the varsity. I'm staying on for a postgraduate year before college. I won't be eligible to play, but I may get to coach a little this season."

Why hadn't Jeff told her that? Chips wondered. *Well, why would you have expected him to?* she lectured herself. *Have you ever been friendly enough to encourage him to tell you about himself?*

Kristen was bobbing around the group like a moth at a light bulb while Ryan and Jeff stuck to soccer. Chips felt oddly grateful that Jeff was giving no indication that he had any connection with her at all—and oddly annoyed that he was treating her no differently from any of the other new faces.

Once she felt confident that Jeff wouldn't stand there and tell Ryan he was her house-sitter, she slipped into the blackness beyond the firelight and walked to the edge of the water, fighting her feeling of disappointment at a lot of the behavior she left behind. The harbor lapped at her toes as she strolled back toward the island, which now lay like a black, beached whale against the lighter gray summer sky. When she saw the yellow light deep in the black shape she didn't even bother to go back for Ryan. She knew he would say again that it was the skipper and whatever he was doing was none of her business. He was right, and Chips knew it.

The dunes that separated her from the fire distorted the music and voices. When she finally heard Ryan's voice calling her, it sounded full of annoyance.

"Be right there," she yelled back, hurrying through the grassy dunes. Suddenly she slammed into someone, who grabbed her as she fell forward toward the sliding sand.

6

As she pitched sideways, gasping in surprise, a pair of arms caught her, bringing her back to her feet and against his chest.

"Well, here she is," said Kristen.

"What the heck were you doing on the other side of the dunes?" Jeff asked, letting go of her as she shook him off.

- "I went for a walk while you and Ryan talked soccer, that's all."

What the heck were you and Kristen doing out here in the dunes, she wanted to ask, trudging along with them, knowing full well what they were doing and hating herself for the pang of jealousy she felt.

"I like the island," she added.

"So I'm beginning to notice," Jeff said.

The three of them finished the walk in silence. Then Ryan spotted them approaching and ran up to join them. Chips knew he'd be angry, but before he could open his mouth, she offered a sincere apology.

"Really, Ryan, I never thought I'd be missed. I just went down to the water. I hope I haven't made everyone late."

"Gate closes in ten minutes!" someone yelled in answer, and everyone scurried to pack the cars.

Kristen took Jeff's arm while Ryan moved away with Chips, shaking his head. "Did she tell you any pirate stories?" he asked, and then pretended to double over as Chips gave him a punch in the ribs.

Jeff did not answer.

Jeff's Jeep and most of the others continued through the parking lot and back into town while the couples that Chips was with lagged behind, arguing about where else they could go. Chips's heart sank at the thought of having to tell Ryan to take her home. But it was late, she'd promised her parents, and she was tired of his boisterous friends.

"Sometimes I forget what a kid you are," he said with a snicker when they were finally alone in his car.

Chips bristled. "I am not a kid! I'm old enough to know when I've had enough, that's all. And most of your friends aren't!" Chips paused. "I like being with you," she added softly, "but I've just had enough."

They drove back to Blueberry Lane in silence and pulled into the driveway, but another half hour went by before she reluctantly got out of the car. Ryan Kennedy had a way of turning on the charm that made her forget the problems they seemed to be having more and more of—problems she was willing to overlook the minute those blue eyes looked into hers.

*　　*　　*

Tuesday it rained just as Ryan had said it would, great sheets of wind-whipped water blowing across the lawn from the bay. Chips set up a makeshift classroom at the kitchen table where she laid out her charts and paper for the class.

She tied the most common knots around the chair backs to

serve as examples for Amy and Lauren. Soon both girls were showing considerable skill at tying their own.

Mrs. Jimmerson was home for the rest of the week to pack for the trip and prepare the household for their departure. "Jeff's here," she said, pulling on her foul weather gear and dashing out the door while Chips watched the two blurry figures, distorted by the rain on the window, head for the garage apartment.

Chips's thoughts turned to how shocked she'd been by plowing into Jeff at the beach party. Too shocked to think about why he had wanted to know what she was looking at when, in fact, she had been looking directly at the spot on the island where she had seen him. Not once, but twice.

With a great deal of effort, she turned back to the table and lost herself in the knots, demonstrating the square knot, bowline, and clove hitch until a dripping Jeff Taylor opened the back door in search of a screw driver. Lauren and Amy made it abundantly clear that it was far more exciting to get a few lessons in knots from an eighteen-year-old boardsailor than from Chips, and she sat back, amused, as they flirted and showed him what they'd been practicing.

He took it in stride—did he take *everything* in stride?—and stayed long enough to show them a trick for remembering each knot. Then he patted Chips on the shoulder. "This is Chips's territory. She knows every bit as much as I do. She'll turn you both into experts."

He winked at her, at least she thought he had, and went back outside. More surprising than that, Chips did not see him again for several days. He seemed to vanish from her life as calmly as he had plowed into it. Finally an exasperated Amy asked Mrs. Jimmerson about him and then informed Lauren that *their* "Mr. Perfection" had taken another caretaking job.

During his absence, they stocked the garage apartment with food, as the weeds continued to sprout in the perennial bed and the girls became comfortable and secure with the boat. Not wanting to risk a change in their positive attitude, Chips kept them in the shallow basin. Bug Light had no teenage visitors that week, and more than once Chips thought about how relieved the skipper probably was.

Chips and Ryan were having their ups and downs, and she worked at convincing herself that Ryan's lack of consideration was not important. Whenever she saw him, his blue eyes continued to make her melt, even though he kept pressuring her to stay out later than she was supposed to. She loved his sense of humor and self-assurance, though it turned occasionally on kids he thought weren't up to his level. More than once she vowed to talk to him about his selfishness, always wanting his own way . . . but she always put it off till their next date.

Even her parents seemed concerned about her "infatuation," as much as they liked Ryan. Chips and her family had agreed that they would spend Saturday, the last day before the Denver medical convention, as a family. But as they lolled around on the sand, she could tell that the one-big-happy-family-on-the-beach-towel scene was leading to something significant.

She was rubbing tanning lotion into her arms when her father cleared his throat.

"Chips, darling, since we're leaving tomorrow, I think we'd better go over a few things."

Why did it sound as though he were about to pull out a sheet numbered one to ten?

"When we made arrangements to be gone for three days, Ryan was not part of the picture. You know we trust you implicitly." He looked at her almost apologetically while Chips wondered if their trust were so implicit why they were having this pep talk at all.

"You've always been so scornful of romance . . . " her mother added.

"Frankly, we didn't anticipate your becoming involved with Ryan when we made plans to leave you here with Mrs. Porter."

"And I, for one, didn't give a thought to how close in age you are to Jeff."

"*Romance . . . involved . . .* " Chips looked from one anxious face to the other, knowing that in a minute they'd start in with the growing-up-before-our-very-eyes bit. Before either parent had a chance, she drew them into a hug.

"Ryan and I enjoy each other, but I wouldn't say we're involved."

"And," she added, "neither of you will get anything done in Colorado if you keep worrying about me. Save your energy, worry about the house. I promise, I'll stick to the rules. Besides, Jeff is dating Kristen Satterfield and I couldn't compete with that even if I wanted to, which I do not. Just watching him around here must convince you of how seriously he takes his work. As far as *I'm* concerned, he's the caretaker in the apartment, and I know as far as he's concerned, I'm a klutzy kid under the wing of Mrs. Porter."

Her parents were smiling, but her father patted her knee. "Now about your sailing. . . . Classes are fine, but I want it understood that you will touch base with Jeff when you're going out. Give him a rough idea of when you'll be back every afternoon."

Chips could feel her face flush. "I don't need a baby-sitter. Mrs. Porter never asks . . . "

"Mrs. Porter has an ill sister to worry about, and besides, when we went away before we were usually as close as Plymouth. I want your word that you will let both of them know your schedule."

"You have my word." She squelched the urge to salute and quickly swallowed the rest of her brownie.

*   *   *

Ryan called after dinner to suggest a sail the following day. "I realize it's your boat"—he laughed—"but I thought we could use some time together."

"No beach party?"

"How about the island, instead? I can impress you with how much I learned last Saturday?"

Chips was elated. "I'd love to sail out there. I've been in the basin all week. Ryan, I'm not sure we should beach there, though," she added thinking of her encounter with the skipper in the post office.

"Why don't we just wait and see. If there's any sign of life, pirate life, that is, we'll go somewhere else."

"Boy, have you changed your tune," she replied.

"Come on, all that was ages ago. I was hoping you'd forgotten all about it, too."

She laughed. "To be perfectly honest, I was hoping if I didn't talk about it anymore that's exactly what you'd think!"

Sunday at noon, with First Parish's bells tolling the hour, Jeff arrived, not in the family Jeep Wagoneer, but on his ten-speed bike. During the Jimmersons' absence, he would have the use of their car, and the back pack slung across his shoulders seemed adequate to contain all the clothes he needed.

He stuck his head in the kitchen just long enough to announce his arrival, then disappeared up into the apartment.

Chips found it mildly irritating that even having to use a bike—albeit a sleek racing model—instead of a racy sports car like Ryan's or the Taylors' Jeep didn't seem to bother him at all. But then, she hardly needed to remind herself, nothing seemed to bother him.

While Dr. Jimmerson went up to go over some last-minute details with Jeff and tell him that Chips would be out in the boat all day, Chips greeted Ryan who had deftly slid his low, green car between the Jimmersons' and Mrs. Porter's.

Ryan suggested that he wait out at the boathouse while she said good-bye to her parents. Finally, the airport limousine arrived.

With final promises to obey the rules, Chips hugged and kissed her parents, promised she'd write to her sister, wished them a safe trip, then turned toward the boathouse.

Ryan was lounging against the boathouse impatiently.

She opened the boathouse, pointing out the key on the wall to Ryan while she picked up two lifejackets. His eyes fell on the stowed sailboard. "I didn't know you had a Windsurfer."

She looked at the red, white, and blue nylon wrapped around the mast. "It's Melissa's," she heard herself answer. A lie, an outright lie. She just couldn't tell him the truth. If he found out that Jeff Taylor was watching the house for three days and the sailboard belonged to him, he might think that she was even more immature for needing a "baby-sitter" while her parents were gone.

She hurried Ryan out of the shed and back onto the dock. Once they had rowed the dinghy to the Lightning, all they had to do was hoist the sail and lower the centerboard, and they were under way.

Chips busied herself with the tiller and loose gear as Ryan pulled on the halyard, the line to hoist the mainsail up the mast. As soon as the tip slid snugly on the top, Ryan cleated the loose end with his newly learned expertise, then opened his mouth to say something to Chips.

Before he could say a word, the halyard strained, then let go with a snap. The boom came crashing down to the deck, and the sail fell lifelessly over the side into the water.

Chips, more surprised than angry, grabbed Ryan's arm. "Some sailor you are, Kennedy! Now the darn thing will drip on us till it dries. Haul it up again and, this time, cleat it tightly!"

Ryan's voice was devoid of humor. "Chips, the halyard snapped in two. It's not my fault. The whole thing has separated—come and look, and don't blame me!"

Chips moved up to the mast, her mouth falling open at the sight of the line, dangling down from the top of the mast. She stood up on the deck and touched the ragged end with her fingers. "Ryan, someone cut my line. Don't you think I'd know if my halyard were so worn it was about to split?"

"Come on, Chips. You don't expect me to buy that!"

No, I don't, she thought sourly. He looked closely as well. "There's no sign of its being cut. This is all frayed."

"I'm telling you," she argued, "someone deliberately cut this partway through to make it break."

Ryan shrugged his shoulders. "Are you going to tell me the

evil skipper came over here in the dead of night and is trying to scare you away from the island? Come on!"

"All I'm trying to tell you is that *my* boat does not have frayed lines."

"And your boat is obviously not going anywhere either," he added moodily. "So much for our private picnic."

Chips looked at him, pushing the apprehension aside. "Help me unrig the mast and we can take the Whaler. How about that?"

The idea of shooting across the bay in a motorboat seemed to cheer him up, and after nearly another half-hour of pulling off the sail and dragging the line into the dinghy, they rowed back to the shore, got the key to the Whaler, transferred the lunch, and were underway. Replacing the line, even worrying about it, could wait, Chips thought to herself.

They flew over the swells of the bay, reaching the lighthouse in less than fifteen minutes. "You must admit, there are advantages to gasoline engines," he shouted over the roar of the motor.

Chips laughed and cupped her hand over her brow to shade her eyes as they came within yards of Bug Light. Ryan slowed the engine. "Go ahead and look for your decoy," he said. "I know darn well you will anyway."

The ladder was empty, and she sighed. "There *was* one up there. There was, Ryan, a week ago last Friday, and you'll never convince me otherwise."

He shrugged his shoulders and concentrated on bringing the boat aground. Chips was the first one out, using the now-exposed cinderblock to secure the line. By the time they had carried the blanket and basket up to the sand, Chips was ready for a swim—but Ryan pulled her into a hug instead.

He had thought to bring a radio and, finding the right station, they sat with their arms around each other listening to the music. "I'm glad we're not at Outer Beach."

"So am I," she replied, enjoying the tingling feeling she got where his hands brushed her fingers. The sun on her bathing suit grew intense, but Chips was too content to move.

Ryan's tender kisses made her feel as warm on the inside as she was on the outside, and she lost her train of thought, thinking he was probably the best kisser in Snug Harbor. Not that she had much to compare him to.

When they got around to eating, the food was warm, the soda positively hot. "That's what you get for distracting me." She laughed as he made a face after one swallow. "How about a swim?"

They walked to the water hand-in-hand and then dove in under the watchful eyes of the soaring sea gulls. When they had finally stopped swimming and were standing in the water waist-deep, Ryan kissed Chips again—but they were kisses she no longer recognized. He was almost hurting her.

She broke away sharply.

"I thought you were glad we didn't go to Outer Beach, that we could be over here by ourselves," Ryan said looking into her eyes.

"I am. Of course I am. I enjoy being with you more than anything."

"Then why won't you let me show you how I feel, Chips? That's why we're here." He grabbed her roughly and tried to kiss her again.

Chips Jimmerson knew a line when she heard one. "Ryan Kennedy, you don't have to *show* me anything! We're here to have a good time, not get into a wrestling match. I want to show you the cove and the pines . . . and be with you, Ryan."

"I can't believe you. When are you going to grow up?" he said acidly, moving out of the water.

"And this is your idea of acting grown-up? Ryan, give me a break. I'm not ready for anything heavy with you and I'm beginning to wonder if I ever want to be."

He turned his head. "What do you mean with *me*? What are you trying to say?"

"I mean I *like* you, I like you a lot, but I don't know if that's enough for more than what we share right now."

Ryan looked at her tenderly but she saw something cold in his eyes that told her he did not take kindly to someone's rebuffing him.

Chips caught up with him and gave him a light hug. "You think I'm ruining it because you want too much! Oh, Ryan, let's not fight. Can't we just enjoy each other?"

He nodded reluctantly. "Yeah, I guess we can try. How about showing me the cove?"

Marching off in search of the skipper did not exactly lift her spirits, but it gave them both something else to think about.

The tide was coming in, covering their tracks in the mud flats as they rounded the island. Ryan made a face as the black sandy soil squished up between their toes. First she took him up the patch to the top of the bluff and pointed out the spot where she had been standing in the dark, their first night on Outer Beach. She did not mention that she had observed Jeff Taylor right below where they were now standing.

By the time they backtracked into the cove, the tidal pools were filling. "The skipper's boat was shoved right in there," she exclaimed, pointing out the empty patch of sand deep in the growth of beach plum. "Can you see how the branches are broken?"

Ryan nodded. "I can also see why this is a great spot to party. We're completely hidden."

"Except for lights," she added. "I've seen the lights over here twice." Beneath her feet, the twigs were digging into the arch of her foot and she bent over, wishing she'd kept on her Topsiders. Her fingers pushed aside the object jabbing her, but as she looked down she cried out in shock.

"Ryan! Look at this." She drew a gold charm bracelet, dripping with mud and silt, out of the mud.

While Ryan stood looking at her, she darted out of the inlet to find water that was deep enough to rinse it off. When he caught up with her, he was breathless. "What are you doing?" he demanded, grabbing her arm as she turned to him.

"It's Kristen Satterfield's," she gasped. "I'm sure of it! She had it on at the beach party . . . Look"—as fast as she could, Chips moved the 14-karat gold charms through her fingers—"here's the miniature crown for Homecoming and here's a medallion with her monogram."

Ryan was studying the engraving. "It's Kristen's all right, I've seen it on her wrist a hundred times."

Chips's eyes were open their widest. "The skipper isn't poaching lobsters, he's part of the robberies that have been going on in town! I know it. This is proof. He probably hides right in there—maybe all the loot is buried right where we were looking. No wonder he was so angry with me and the kids. That sliced halyard *was* a warning!"

A shudder made her tremble, and she turned back to look at the inlet. "We've got to get off this island!"

Ryan was quiet long enough to let Chips finish, but as she started to rush back along the shoreline, he held her back and began to laugh. "For heaven's sake, Chips, slow down. This is Pilgrim Cove. *You* may not want a heavy relationship, but Kristen is no kid! She probably lost her bracelet when she was here with Jeff Taylor."

Chips's cheeks burned. She felt as though Ryan had knocked the breath out of her, but she continued walking resolutely back to their blanket. She refused to acknowledge the painful stab she felt in her chest at the thought of Kristen and Jeff together. She knew he was familiar with the island . . . Chips did not want to believe the explanation could be so simple. "What more proof do you need? I saw a decoy at the lighthouse, I saw one in his boat, and now I have a very valuable piece of jewelry from the same spot—from the skipper's hideout."

"Hideout? Chips, listen to how dumb you sound. The police will tell you the same thing. Even your father told you this has been a *hang*out, not a hideout, for years."

He sat down next to her, his ruddy face flushed with trying to make her listen.

"You want to play Nancy Drew? Okay. Here's the scenario: Jeff Taylor moves to town, moves right next door to Kristen Satterfield, a girl very used to getting whatever she wants. She collects boys like she collects those charms, and she obviously brought Jeff over here to show him Clark's Island."

"With her bracelet on?" Chips asked, subdued.

"She wears the stupid thing day and night."

Chips's mood turned black. Of course Ryan would know how much she wore it. Kristen and Mary Thompson were inseparable. They spent every weekend last year double-dating with Ryan and whomever Kristen liked at the moment. That much Chips knew. And at the moment, Jeffrey Taylor was the one Kristen wanted, Chips had seen it with her own eyes.

She drew her knees up to her chin, trying to decide which was more depressing, the fact that Ryan wouldn't believe her or the thought of Kristen throwing herself at Jeff . . . or the disagreeable fact that she was thinking of Jeff at all.

She leaned over and looked at her date. "I don't want to stay on this island another minute, and whether you like it or not, Ryan, I'm going to the police. I've been talked out of it for the last time."

She moved around frantically, scooping up the hamper, towels, and shoes into her overburdened arms until she was so weighted down she could not have walked out to their boat if she wanted to.

Ryan began to laugh, and the more he laughed the angrier she got. "Make fun of me if you want to, but the police have got to see this bracelet. They may be over there in their offices just waiting for a clue."

Ryan took half the load, leaving her to form a wake as she plowed through the hip-deep water. "Waiting for a clue? You know what they'll think we've been doing over here. At least call Kristen first. If she's not home, then *you* can go to the police."

He was still laughing as they got into the boat and started the motor. Chips eased the Whaler through the stretch between the lighthouse and the island and then let Ryan steer over to the channel markers and straight down the basin to the town landing.

Mr. Perfection, she thought, was fresh and sarcastic and full of self-importance. Even his body language as he stood at the wheel with his shoulders jauntily thrown back told her he was determined to show her once again that he was right by proving her suspicions groundless.

As they approached the busy harbor, Ryan cut the engine back and Chips again took over, maneuvering her boat gently through the vessels at anchor until she nudged the town pier. With the skill that comes from practice, she executed a perfect docking maneuver while Ryan jumped out and secured the bow and stern to the pilings.

Chips sped ahead to the harbor master's office on the edge of the water. After asking for the phone book and getting permission for a local call, she let Ryan dial the Satterfields. No answer, not even after ten rings.

"They may be at the beach, Chips."

She looked at Ryan. "You agreed." He looked as though he regretted it.

With Ryan at her heels, she turned from the office and sped through the bustling village center, feeling suddenly self-conscious as she realized she was wearing only a bathing suit and boat shoes.

Ryan, who was less single-minded, had thought to bring their shirts, and as they trotted across Bay Road, past the movie theater and up a side street, he pulled his polo shirt over his head and handed Chips her yellow top.

The two of them arrived at the police station just as Chips was shooting her arms into her sleeves. Ryan held the door for her.

The sergeant at the desk came over to the counter as they let the screen door slam behind them.

"Problem, kids?" the officer asked brightly.

Chips nodded, and Ryan shook his head. The officer looked from one to the other. "Which is it?"

Chips dropped the bracelet on the counter. "I found this about an hour ago on Clark's Island, in Pilgrim Cove. I have reason to believe it might be stolen and possibly part of the robberies going on lately."

The sergeant lifted her eyebrows. "It belongs to Kristen Satterfield on Colony Drive," Chips added, relieved to see that the officer was taking her seriously.

"John Satterfield's house, Twenty-four Colony Drive," Ryan put in.

"I have also run into a man in an unregistered boat out there. The boat's a little bigger than a Boston Whaler—a guy in his late twenties, dark curly hair, beard"—she turned to Ryan— "a little taller than he is."

The policewoman nodded and took the bracelet into an adjoining office as Chips and Ryan watched her bend over a plainclothed man at a desk. He looked back and then came toward them. "I'm Detective Witter, can you tell me more about this guy and his boat?"

With "I told you so" written all over her face, Chips looked at Ryan and then described in detail everything she could remember about the skipper. Both officers were nodding, thanking her for her time, and then advising the two of them to stay out of trouble and leave everything to the police.

"Clark's Island is no place for somebody your age, and no matter what this guy is up to, harmless or not, you'd be smart to steer clear of him."

Chips felt her ears burn. She didn't dare look at Ryan.

"What about the bracelet?"

The detective moved it with his fingers. "I congratulate you on your honesty. Since you seem to know the Satterfield girl, would you like to return it?"

Chips blinked. "You don't need it as evidence from their housebreak?"

The sergeant looked at the detective and smiled. "Everybody in this town is on edge. We don't have any report of a robbery at the Satterfields', and to my knowledge they haven't had any problems." He gave her a look that added silently *except with their daughter sneaking onto Clark's Island.* "My guess is that Miss Satterfield was picnicking on the island just like you two. It's always been a popular spot, you know."

I know, I know, Chips told herself, thinking that Kristen would probably have been doing a lot more than picnicking. She took the bracelet back from the officers.

The last thing Chips wanted was to have Ryan deposit her on Colony Drive when he entertained Kristen with stories of Nancy Drew's overactive sense of the dramatic.

"*I'll* see that she gets it," Chips said—as much to Ryan as to the officers.

7

Chips knew it was coming, but Ryan kept his temper until they were back in the boat and heading for the Jimmersons'. "I hope you're satisfied. I really mean it. Chips, you've got to get this out of your system. Those officers made me feel like a dumb kid playing cops and robbers. Why the heck can't you just lay off and enjoy the summer like everyone else?"

It was a question she couldn't answer. Why, oh, why wasn't Ryan able to understand? The sad part was, he didn't seem to want even to try. Chips looked at him as he stood at the wheel, the wind blowing the hair back from his handsome face. She also knew that molding herself into whatever it was that Ryan wanted her to be would never work. She just could never be happy unless she was herself.

She knew that the whole skipper mess had embarrassed him from the beginning, and she hoped for a minute that it was just because he was used to being with Mary Thompson, the kind of girl who wanted nothing more from life than to be able to bask in Ryan's glow. But somehow Chips knew there was more to it than that. Just because he hadn't seen the decoy, why wouldn't he believe that she had? Did he care about her at all, or was he only concerned about what people thought of him?

Chips turned away, letting the rush of wind blow the hot tears from her cheeks. Maybe she *had* imagined it—the one on the ladder, anyway. Maybe the skipper *was* a poacher or a down-on-his-luck lobsterman. Anyway it was none of her business.

Maybe Jeff and Kristen were spending all their time together. That was none of her business either.

They managed to be cordial to each other as they docked the boat and put the key back in the shed. Ryan was acting very thoughtfully and giving Chips a hand with the hamper and towels, but he didn't have much to say until they were back at the house.

Mrs. Porter's parking place was empty; Chips hoped Jeff wouldn't suddenly appear and start taking his house-sitting job too seriously.

Ryan turned to Chips and brushed the sea-dampened hair from her forehead. "So what do we do now, my beautiful detective? Are you going to ask me to stay awhile, so we can have a chance to enjoy some *rare* privacy?"

Chips paused. Why was it that Ryan always seemed to make what should have been a compliment sound like an insult? She was tempted, but then Ryan continued. "Or do you have to rush inside to take notes on this afternoon's find? Listen, I'm really sorry that I was so crabby, but I just wish you'd stop tearing around all over the place and acting so sure of yourself!"

"I'm usually right."

"Not this time!" There was enough irritation in his voice for Chips to stop. She shook her head.

"We could go for a swim or call out for a pizza, it's after six."

"Ryan," she began quietly, "you know I can't."

"Who's to know?"

She blinked hard and looked up in surprise. "Who's to know? *I'm* to know. I think you better go, now, before we say things we'll be sorry for."

Ryan didn't argue, but when he kissed her, she could tell he did it kind of mechanically, as though he thought he had to. Instead of the contentment that she usually felt when they parted, her chest ached, a lead weight seemed to settle behind her ribs.

Earlier he'd mentioned there was going to be a beach party Monday night, but now neither of them brought it up.

This time she didn't wait to watch the car wind down Blueberry Lane. As Ryan turned on the ignition, Chips picked up the hamper and went into the empty house.

She kept herself busy with dinner and replacing the Lightning's severed line with a supply in the basement until well after dark. At eight thirty, after changing into jeans and a cotton sweater she left to put the line in the boathouse, intending to let her students help rerig in the morning. Growing pains. Her mother would have said she was having growing pains, and Chips smiled in the dark as her bare feet slid on the cropped grass. She missed her parents already.

She wanted to shake Ryan by the shoulders and tell him he wasn't living up to her expectations. That was what was making her chest ache, she guessed, the sad realization that Ryan wasn't any more or less than just Ryan Kennedy. "Mr. Perfection" was turning out to be a figment of her imagination.

The waxing moon was rising, casting broken reflections on the quiet bay. With the line over her arm, she slipped the boathouse key from its hiding spot, and entered the shed, completely forgetting about Jeff's sailboard.

Entering the dark interior, she knocked into the metal mast, and let out a painful gasp. The sailboard went crashing over in the dark, taking with it the stack of aluminum beach chairs, a metal watering can, and the oars to the dinghy. It was not the first time she wished her father had put a light in the boathouse. She hopped painfully on one foot, said "darn" under her breath, and rubbed her shin. Then she fell back against the dark wall.

Suddenly the white beam of a marine flashlight sliced the dank room. Chips cringed and then sat, as the glare caught her face, pale with shock. Her pupils opened like black pools, but before she could scream a hand grabbed her shoulder and she found herself being yanked to her feet.

"What the heck are you doing?" Jeff demanded, pulling and then supporting her as she limped onto the grass.

"You don't have to yell at me."

"Yell at you? You're lucky I didn't just call the police and have them search the shed. Do you have any idea how much noise you made?"

"Me? It was your stupid sailboard attacking me."

They stood still for a minute. Relief flooded through Chips while her would-be rescuer sighed. Her shin no longer hurt, but the gentle support of Jeff's arms was as pleasant as his flashlight had been rude, and she kept her weight against him.

"Are you all right?"

Reluctantly she agreed that she was, stepped back from him, and stood on her own. "You wouldn't have called the police?"

Jeff shook his head. "No. I knew you came back with Ryan, but honestly, Chips. . ."

"Honestly, nothing. I don't need to report my every move to you."

"Not unless you intend to take the boathouse with you."

Even in the dark, she could sense the easygoing Taylor manner returning. "Hard day with the soccer captain?"

"I'm not in the mood for your teasing, Jeff. I've made a fool of myself enough today, and one run-in with the police " She stopped, wishing she'd bitten off her words one sentence sooner. Her move back to the brick path and up toward the house was not quick enough. Jeff was beside her again before she'd gone five feet.

"You'd better finish that sentence, Chips."

"It's none of your business."

"From now until Wednesday, it's my business. Like it or not."

"Well, don't report me to Denver," she began. "I recently had a run-in with a boat owner who told me to mind my own business. The guy who stopped me from his car the night I walked to Nana's. Remember?"

"Yes, I remember. You looked scared to death."

"Well, I wasn't. He operates an unregistered boat I found in Pilgrim Cove, that's all. I took Ryan over there today for a picnic."

The easygoing manner vanished, replaced by a tenseness as he listened to her.

"Ryan and I started to sail . . . but my halyard was frayed and it snapped, so we took the Whaler instead . . . I found your friend Kristen's charm bracelet in the cove. . . I thought my line was cut on purpose and that her bracelet was stolen—you know, part of all these robberies and as usual I made a complete fool of myself."

She was surprised to find herself fighting tears. "We called the Satterfields, and when there wasn't any answer, I made Ryan come with me to the police. They didn't take me seriously, just like Ryan. Just like you. They didn't even want the bracelet. In fact, it's up in my room. Since Miss Homecoming Queen probably lost it out there with you, Jeff, I thought you'd want to give it back to her." Chips's voice broke. "There," she finished, "I hope you're satisfied."

They reached the kitchen steps, and she didn't need the back porchlight to see the concern etched in Jeff's face. His tone of voice was even, but low and demanding.

"Look, I don't know who this guy is or what he's up to, but I want your word you'll stay off the island while I'm responsible for you."

"You're not responsible for me! You've been hired to watch the property. Mrs. Porter and I can manage just fine, Jeff, and if it weren't for the stupid robberies all over town you wouldn't even be here."

"But there *are* robberies all over town and you *are* worth more than any jewelry or silver, Chips. All I'm asking is that you stick close to home while I'm here."

"I'm not a kid."

"No, you're not. Sometimes I wonder if you know just how fast you are moving. That island is no place for you and Ryan Kennedy—and he knows it, even if you don't."

Chips looked into his brown eyes, confused. Was he worried about her snooping around a potentially dangerous lobster poacher or her behavior with a seventeen-year-old guy? And what about *his* island escapades with a seventeen-year-old Homecoming Queen?

Jeff's voice softened. "I know you think you can take care of yourself."

She opened her mouth to protest, but his warm fingers pressed lightly against her lips to keep her still. "Just don't spend the next three days trying to prove it. Okay?"

She was so surprised by the thrill she felt at his touch that when he took his hand away she simply nodded.

If Jeff noticed, he did not let on. He simply waited for her to enter the kitchen and then turned toward his garage apartment. Chips walked through her empty house with her mind spinning, finally settling in the den in the front, off the living room.

It was only nine o'clock, so after ten minutes of a boring television program, she flicked off the set and turned to the book shelves lining the outside wall.

The large paned windows across the front of the house were open, letting in the sweet honeysuckle smell from the tangle of bushes just outside. Chips settled into the couch, looking up from her book only occasionally whenever a June bug butted against the screen in an effort to reach the lighted room.

She had scanned Melissa's old collection of Nancy Drew mysteries and had chosen one about a lighthouse. Maybe, she thought with a smile, it would tell her how to recognize clues or convince doubting boyfriends to take her seriously.

Skimming the pages, she found herself engrossed in the story and laughing at the heavy weather, foggy nights, and strangers in the shadows. When the scratching began on the screen, she didn't look up at first because she thought more bugs were flapping against the mesh.

The couch was against the wall where the window was, so she had her back to the darkness. When she heard the sound again it was not the *ping* of a bug, but a long drawn out scrape starting at the edge and stopping suddenly behind her right ear—like the slice of a knife through the metal screen.

In the time it took for her heart to stop and then begin to race again, the fine hairs along her arms rose in gooseflesh. She bit her bottom lip to hold in a scream and turned around slowly. The window screen was intact.

Behind her, outside the screen, the night was black. And as she tried to whip her brain into action, her hands clutched the edge of the couch, her fists bunching up the fabric as she clutched at it.

Could she hear breathing? Who was out there? A prowler thinking the house was empty? Or the skipper who knew she was there?

When the scratch came again, this time on her left, Chips was beyond thinking rationally. She bolted from the couch and darted into the living room, which was as dark as the lawn beyond. To give herself time to catch her breath, she leaned against the wall dividing the room from the den, peering out into the night.

It was not her eyes that turned her terror to fury. It was her nose. Mingled with the summer sweet honeysuckle was the unmistakable aroma of tomato sauce and mozzarella; and just as her brain clicked *pizza*, ghostly, tremulous stage whispers on the lawn began to coo, "Chiiiiiiiips, oh Chiiiiiiiips."

Before the voices came again, she was at the front door, yanking it open so savagely it slammed against the wall while she pushed through the screen door. Barely discernible shadows were coming into view, from gray to black, in three sizes. A couple of kids she recognized from the beach finally stopped howling her name. Ryan himself was holding the square cardboard box of pizza.

She was about to use every curse she'd ever heard when the familiar beam of the Jimmersons' marine light caught them. It held Ryan, frozen in surprise until he jumped, dropping the pizza at his feet.

"How does that feel, Kennedy?" came the authoritative voice out of the dark.

The relentless glare moved to the girl and she began to back away. "I told you this was a stupid idea. Chips, they made me come along. Now we're going to get arrested, Peter," she whined to her date as he threw his arm up to shield his eyes.

For long, agonizing moments, Chips's heart felt lodged in her throat. Once her pulse had slowed to a more normal rate, she moved to the door and flicked on the small outside light.

"Pick up your pizza and eat it on your own property," was all Jeff said as the three of them stared at him. Ryan was the first to recover.

"Taylor?" he mumbled as though he could not quite believe whom he was seeing.

Chips cringed, waiting for Jeff's long-overdue explanation to the kids that he was the caretaker. She caught Jeff's eye and looked away.

"I could easily have been the police, and there's enough tension in this town that they might have shot first and asked questions later."

The girl gasped again.

"I want you off the Jimmerson property. Now." Jeff stood rock still while Ryan's friends mumbled that they'd see him at the car and disappeared into the shadows.

Ryan picked up the pizza with deliberate cool and looked at Chips. "We only came over here to get you. You're so darned hung up on playing detective, I thought you'd love a little mystery of your own." His voice began to drip with sarcasm. "I had no idea I'd be interrupting anything. No wonder you wouldn't let me stay after our little fiasco this afternoon. You had another date! Boy, you really put one over on me at the beach today."

Jeff's face clouded, and his knuckles turned white where he gripped the handle of the light.

"Jeff, here, is the caretaker, Ryan. My parents hired him to watch the house while they're gone. He's staying in the apartment over the garage."

Ryan looked from Jeff back to her. "You expect me to believe that?"

Chips took a sharp breath. "Frankly, no. You don't believe half of what I say most of the time, anyway. I don't expect you to act any differently now."

"Take your dinner and join your friends," Jeff said it as though it were Ryan's last chance.

"I think Chips can speak for herself," Ryan shot back.

"You'd better go," was the soft answer she gave him.

"Are you coming?"

"No, Ryan, I'm not. Having the life scared out of me is not my idea of a joke. I'm tired." . . . *of you,* she wanted to add, but didn't. The pain, heavy and deep, returned to her chest as Ryan sighed.

Ryan turned on his heels and, with an exaggerated swagger, walked into the shadows toward the car.

In the distance, Chips heard the motor roar into the night as she stared out into the dark bay at the flashing beacon of Bug Light.

She bit her lip again, not out of fear but to suppress the sobs welling up from the ache in her ribs, and she kept walking until she was beyond the range of the door light. Tears, faster than she could blink them away, filled her eyes. She prayed Jeff had gone back to his apartment.

At that moment, all she wanted was to be by herself and brood about how much she hated Ryan for his immaturity, for his nasty insinuations, for the hurt she felt. She did not dare turn around for fear Jeff was there, watching, as always.

She'd been so smug in front of him that first evening, marching off to meet Ryan. For a moment, she couldn't think of anything she'd done right in the presence of Jeffrey Taylor.

When he caught up with her in the dark, Chips was not surprised. She rubbed her eyes roughly with the sleeve of her sweater.

"It's tough, isn't it, when somebody you really like doesn't live up to your expectations. Sort of hits you like a punch in the ribs."

"What does?" she managed to whisper.

"When you get hurt by someone."

Without a thought for what she was doing, Chips Jimmerson turned, buried her face in the warm hollow of Jeffrey Taylor's shoulder, and cried herself dry. It felt so good being snuggled up against the scratchiness of his wool sweater. He smelled wonderful: like a combination of mint and fresh soap.

When she was composed enough to start to feel embarrassed, she straightened up, aware that Jeff had wrapped his arms protectively around her as she clung to his neck.

"I'm sorry," came the apology muffled into his sweater. She hiccupped, still pressed against him, and she felt him laugh softly.

He loosened his arms, keeping one around her shoulder as they walked back to the house. "Don't ever be sorry about your feelings, Chips. You'll never get the highs without hitting bottom once in a while. Ryan acts like a real jerk sometimes. Maybe you had him so high on a pedestal he couldn't be what you wanted. Out there on the island or tonight—just now at the window— maybe he was pushing you, trying to mold you into whatever it is he wants."

Chips was back at the front door, looking up into his concerned brown eyes, calmed by the quiet understanding as much as by his arms. "I don't want to be what he wants."

Jeff smiled. "That probably gets to him, too."

She bit her lip, overwhelmed by his insight.

"Will you be all right, now?" he asked gently but a little more impersonally.

She nodded. "Thank you. Thank you for being there. I guess I did need you after all."

With his thumb, he wiped a stray tear from her cheek. "That's what I'm here for."

*　　　*　　　*

After locking the door, Chips went up to her room and slipped into her nightgown. Her room had the same view as the living room directly below, and she stood in the dark at her open window watching the lighthouse.

The honeysuckle scent, fainter at that height came wafting in on the night breeze. Moments ago, she'd been terrified, but now she felt oddly secure. Jeff was right, of course. She had put Ryan on a pedestal.

Jeff, who never once laughed at her, who knew just how awful she felt. . . She remembered how tender his touch had been when he'd wiped away her tears. Her face felt tingly, and slowly Chips closed her eyes, remembering his wonderful, warm smile. Was it possible that she'd been blind to the one person who might be exactly what she was looking for simply because he'd been in her own backyard? With a sigh, Chips looked out again into the dark. Near by the boathouse a beam of the light caught her attention. She knew it was Jeff, conscientiously walking the grounds. The beam swung back in the direction of the dark house, and she was about to turn for bed when it went out.

Chips stood watching. When it came again it was aimed out at the water, hitting the stern of the Lightning. Then it went out again. On, catching the Whaler, off . . . on once more. Her hands turned clammy.

From her second-story window, she fought against thinking the obvious: Jeff was signaling.

*   *   *

She was horrified. But a night which, by rights, should have had her tossing and turning with insomnia, found her sound asleep. The overcast sunrise had failed to wake her and by the time Chips rolled over to look at her clock, it was nearly 10 in the morning.

She threw herself off the mattress, looked at the skies and pulled on khaki shorts and a white polo shirt. Greeting her in the breakfast room, where she sat reading the paper over a cup of coffee, was the welcome sight of Mrs. Porter.

"Good morning, sleepy head!"

Chips grinned. "You should have gotten me up."

The housekeeper shrugged. "No need. Your students don't arrive until noon, and I thought you might need the rest after the big day with your Ryan."

Chips's back stiffened, her voice irritable. "He's not *my* Ryan."

The gentle face of the older woman regarded Chips affection-ately. She nodded. "I'm sorry."

Chips shook her head. "Don't be. Will Jeff be eating with us?"

"Not this morning. He wanted some time to go into town and since I'm here all day, I gave him as much time as he wants. Soon as he got back, he went right out on that sailboard of his. Maybe you and your students will run into him out there."

Chips found herself smiling at the memory of how literal that statement had been two weeks ago. She went into the kitchen in search of a bowl of cereal. In front of the counter, she stopped dead in her tracks and shouted for Mrs. Porter. Her cry was so alarming that the housekeeper jumped from her seat and ran into the kitchen.

"Where did you get that?" Chips demanded as Alice Porter looked from her pale face to the kitchen counter. She picked up the perfectly carved figure of a sitting gull and tried to hand it to Chips.

Chips took it as if it were hot.

"Jeff gave it to me this morning for my sister."

"Your sister? Did he get it from the lighthouse? Did he tell you?"

"The lighthouse? Of course not. What would he have been doing at Bug Light? He carves them, dear. Isn't it beautiful work?"

Chips was nodding dumbly as the housekeeper turned it over. "There's his signature, J.T., in a little oval." She put it back in Chips's icy hands.

"Are you all right, dear?"

The nodding continued. "Yes. Yes, of course. Just surprised that he has so much talent." J.T. in an oval. Her stomach knotted.

As soon as humanly possible, Chips finished nibbling at her cereal, which turned to dust in her throat. Leaving Mrs. Porter in the kitchen, she flew up the back stairs, plopping onto her unmade bed to think.

Out of nowhere comes a boy to house-sit . . . new in town . . . insists that she stay away from the island. Think, darn it, she demanded of herself. She'd seen him out there. *He knew she'd seen him there . . .* his decoy was in the skipper's boat *and on the ladder* whether Ryan Kennedy believed her or not.

Did Jeff know she'd seen any decoys? Desperately she tried to remember, shaking her head against the pillow. No, she hadn't mentioned it.

Sweet, brotherly Jeff . . . handsome, caring Jeff. She shivered. Was that why he had been so affectionate, to get her to open up to him, tell him what she knew? What she suspected?

Chips got off the bed and walked quietly to the attic door, turning the knob with the stealth of a cat burglar. Nearly eleven and the July heat smothered her as she crept up the stairs to the third floor.

The telescope fell against her hip as she pulled it out. She opened the door to the widow's walk, then stood up firmly, balanced the telescope, and focused on the green splash of color in the sparkly bay.

She put her eye to the lens, adjusting it with trembling fingers as she set the sight on open water, the glass dome of the light . . . lower to the pine bluffs . . . the inlet, the beached sailboard—and the red, white, and blue nylon propped against the wild hedge of roses.

8

Chip's mind was in turmoil. Her head spun as she looked through the lens at Jeff's beached sailboard. The tide was coming in, filling the inlet into Pilgrim Cove where Jeff Taylor, no doubt, was at this very moment huddled with the skipper.

Why had she ever told him she'd gone to the police? Were the two of them out there plotting how to move their operation to a safer spot, or, worse . . . she forced her mind to consider it . . . were they discussing what should be done about an overly curious sixteen-year-old sailing instructor?

And why couldn't she come up with something specific so that somebody—anybody, at this point—would believe her? Chips put the telescope away as she wondered to herself what the penalty was for poaching lobsters. Was it considered stealing? A felony . . . like stealing jewelry?

It was a relief to get out of the stifling attic, but Chips came back to the second floor with her mind still whirling. Think!

She knew for a fact that Jeff had watched the Russos' house and they had been robbed. How about the Gordons'? She shook her head, unable to recall. Unsuspected teenage caretaker cases the house, knows precisely where everything is, signals his accomplice in the dead of the night—*just as he did from the end of the dock while he thought I was asleep!*

Chips went down to the kitchen, aware that if she kept up her racing speculation, she'd be feeling frantic by dinner. She was so confused. She kept seeing in her mind's eye the look of genuine concern in Jeff's warm brown eyes as he held her in his arms last night. He acted as though he cared about her. How could he have faked everything so convincingly?

But she had to clear her head. There were students to meet—diversion. With a quick good-bye, Chips left Mrs. Porter, but she did not head straight for the boathouse. Instead she slipped unnoticed across the driveway to the door leading up to the garage apartment. It was unlocked.

Once inside she bounded up the stairs, two at a time, until she was on the landing at the top. The doorknob wouldn't budge. She had expected the door to be locked, but she knew that it had glass panes in it to a level above her waist. Chips pressed her nose up to the mullions, peering through her mother's fringe of curtains into Jeff's temporary quarters.

Dishes sat on the drainboard in the kitchenette; a sailing magazine was open on the couch. Two shirts she recognized as his were flung over a chair. Sloppy, she thought, but then, he's obviously too busy to be neat, too busy with his illegal, clandestine activities. The ache was back behind her ribs, but not just for Jeff. For herself, too. She ached for ever having trusted that brown-eyed boardsailor, for ever thinking he understood her problems and for ever, ever letting him see her as vulnerable as she'd been last night.

Chips twisted away from the window, no longer wanting to look at anything that reminded her of him. In spite of her disappointment and loneliness, she had to harden herself against her feelings. She was never going to allow herself to feel that way again about Jeff. He had lied. He was a traitor. But just as she was turning, her eyes caught the one thing she had come to find. The table beside the couch was set up, littered in fact, with carving tools, paints, and the beginnings of another decoy. *What did you expect?* she asked herself angrily. *Do you think Mrs. Porter made the whole thing up?*

Feeling sadder than she ever had in her life, Chips sank down on the stairs, burying her head in her hands.

"Jeff Taylor," she whispered his name out loud, swallowing the hurt. Part of her wanted to confront him with what she knew—try to make him confess—and part of her kept saying it was all a bad dream and Jeff would straighten everything out.

Pushing herself to her feet, Chips left the steps, wiping her eyes, doing her best to convince herself that she owed Jeff that much. But the idea of listening and trusting him, even with Mrs. Porter in the room, frightened her. Lost in thought, she walked down the path to the beachfront.

As she headed toward the water, remembering that she had to lay out the halyard and sail with her new students, she thought of Detective Witter. What would his reaction be to her new evidence? Evidence of what? That Jeffrey Taylor was an excellent wood carver? Like the evidence that he'd spent time in the cove with Kristen? The pieces to Chips's puzzle could mean one thing as easily as another. Blast him!

Even those troubling thoughts flew from her mind as Chips reached the water. She stared out at the mooring and then, as if she couldn't believe her eyes, she ran to the end of the dock. The Lightning was gone!

Frantically she looked left, then right, following the empty shoreline in both directions. Nothing. Ryan. Was this another joke? A way to get back for last night? Jeff. Had he somehow taken it, sailed away with it? No, she told herself, it hadn't been rigged. It would have to have been towed during the night. More than that—towed by someone who meant business— someone who maybe thought that the frayed halyard had not been warning enough!

Before Chips ran to the house she looked out at Clark's Island. Someone wanted her off of it, and she didn't need a crystal ball now to know it was the skipper *and* Jeff—both of whom were probably out there this minute. Any thoughts of giving Jeff a chance to explain—to come up with a lie—vanished.

While she called the police from the kitchen, she told Mrs. Porter about the Lightning. The officer took down the description and her registration numbers, but he sounded less than optimistic that it would be found soon, given the rash of thefts in the area. Great, she'd have to wait in line like everyone else.

After collecting her wits, deciding not to frighten Mrs. Porter with what she suspected, Chips picked up the phone again. Jason and Kirk Allen, eleven and fourteen, were her students for the week. Town racing champions, they had hired Chips for practice, wanting to sail imaginary courses in an effort to improve their speed.

As upset as she was, it was a simple matter to have them sail their boat from the basin up to the Jimmersons'. When she suggested it, both boys and their mother offered it for the duration of the classes. She thanked them, hoping her Lightning would be back before then.

The first day's lesson was devoted to practicing timing, running over imaginary starting lines, and rounding markers for the summer regattas. Chips had her hands full, but it was a relief to concentrate on something other than her increasingly frightening situation.

As far as either boy was concerned, the only clouds on the horizon were the real ones, which were building into towering, cumulus configurations—ominous, but having the effect of keeping the wind strong and steady. The three of them flew through the channel toward open water, hiking out over the side until they were drenched with sea spray. Chips had not done much laughing and whooping, but the infectious force of the brisk wind and expert helmsmanship made her shout happily with the boys, putting aside her anxiety until they reached the mouth of the harbor and Bug Light. By then, the weather was worsening, the swells soaking them so they agreed to once around and home.

Chips sat back and let the Allen brothers bring their boat around, through the narrows of the island and point for the Jimmersons.

Her only words were those of encouragement and congratulation, but she had bitten her lower lip nearly to the point of bleeding. Jeff's sailboard was gone. But the decoy was back on the ladder.

Kirk kept the sail close hauled for maximum speed; he snapped the boom efficiently as they came about and caught the wind to starboard. The lighthouse fell away behind them within seconds.

Ryan would have told her there was no way to double check what she thought she'd seen midway up the rusty ladder. Nevertheless, Chips had never been so sure about anything in her life. The bird near the railing was carved, not perched, not living, not dead—inanimate, a replica blending perfectly with its fluttering neighbors, up there for a reason known to the skipper and Jeff.

Beneath her wet polo shirt, Chip's heart pounded savagely, so hard she was sure it must be visible. But the boys, engrossed in their sail, were concentrating on trimming the sail and hiking out, so they made it back to port in record time.

Jason brought his boat to Chip's mooring with Kirk on the heaving bow, trying to grab for the bobber as the boat slapped up and down in the rising waters. Spitting salt water, he yelled that he was having a great time.

Both boys brushed off her thanks for the loan of the boat and after securing it, set off on foot for their house.

Now what? Fear clutched at Chip's heart, making her want to run to her room and draw herself up into a tight, safe ball on her bed.

But then it would be dark. Mrs. Porter would be home with her sister. Dear Mrs. Porter who thought Jeff was so charming and thoughtful and concerned, just as Chips had, would go home. And then it wouldn't be safe at all.

She knew what she had to do.

It wasn't until she put the life jackets in the boathouse that she turned to see Jeff's sailboard drying just above the high water line.

He was back.

The wind blew Chip's skin to a dry, salty itch, now hot, now cool as the clouds whipped past the sun. But there was no time for her to shower.

She scanned the property looking for Jeff's bare back in the perennial flower bed, around the boathouse, even in the thicket of honeysuckle. The front door of the Jimmerson house was open, catching the wind, and with the same stealth she'd used on the attic door, Chips gingerly pressed the button on the screen door, letting herself in. Except for the familiar buzz of the vacuum cleaner on the second floor, the house was still. She tiptoed through the living room into the den. Four-thirty. The sun went behind another cloud.

Offering up a silent prayer that Ryan would be home from camp, she dialed his number, pressing the receiver to her ear as it rang four, five, then six times. The familiar voice said "Hello" after the seventh ring.

"Ryan?" Chips whispered harshly.

"Who is this?"

"Chips, Ryan. I'm calling because the decoy is back on the lighthouse steps."

"Great. But you don't need to whisper. I'm sure it can't hear you from way out there."

Though she had expected a reaction like the one she was getting, it stung, making her flush.

"Believe me, I wouldn't be bothering you with this again if I didn't need your help. Listen to me, please. My boat is missing! I used my students' and the decoy is back and I've got another one just like it. Both of them were carved—"

"Save it," he snapped. "Haven't you been through enough with this, Chips?" She could hear him sigh. "I believe you, really, but I don't care if there's half a dozen decoys on the lighthouse. Call the police about your boat. It probably tore from the mooring in the wind last night."

When she spoke, her voice sounded strained and icy. "I just called to see if you'd help me get the decoys to the harbor master. I've known Mr. Ransom all my life and he'll listen." *Even if you won't,* she thought angrily.

"When do you need me?"

"Oh, Ryan," she replied, her hope renewed, "right this minute. We don't have any time to spare."

The pause on the other end of the phone sent a chill of apprehension down her back, and the tone of his voice when Ryan finally answered only made it worse. "Chips," he said quietly, "I thought after last night we were through, you know, that you wouldn't want to see me again. I called Mary—that is, she's back from vacation. We're . . . going out in a few minutes."

He sounded embarrassed and apologetic, and Chips gripped the phone hoping she was right. "Forget it, then. You and Mary have a great evening."

"Be careful. Chips. Don't do anything stupid."

"Ryan," she sighed, "the only stupid thing I ever did was get involved with you."

Before he could reply, she dropped the receiver back on the cradle.

There wasn't time for tears, and she brushed them away with a furious sweep of her salty hand as she went into the kitchen. The vacuum was still running and a glance at the driveway told her Jeff was most likely in his apartment. Both her family's car and Jeff's bike were in plain view.

Her hasty note said only: *Mrs. P—Have taken the Whaler out to look for my Lightning. Don't worry, may be late but home before dark. XXX, C.*

She read it over and then added a postscript to make it look as innocent as possible. *Please tell Jeff before you go so he won't worry.*

She was hardly giving herself away, she thought, since one look at the mooring would tell either of them she was out. She yanked a canvas carryall from the closet, stuffed binoculars and her foul weather slicker into it, looked once around the room, grabbed the decoy from the counter, and sped through the house, out the front door.

After she got the decoys to Mr. Ransom, she had no idea what she'd do. Maybe she could call a friend and spend the night.

Chips had not counted on the change in the weather—a stiff wind of the kind she ordinarily would have avoided. Whitecaps were breaking on the shore as she furiously turned on the engine.

Chips's mistake was immediately apparent to her. Her slicker did nothing to keep her legs dry as the boat slapped across the breaking water. Wave after wave blew across the bow soaking her shorts and legs.

The wind made it impossible to take the time to fasten the jacket, and within minutes her already damp polo shirt was clinging like a flat piece of kelp.

Common sense told her to forget the lighthouse and just go down the channel to the town landing, convince Mr. Ransom to come with her, and let him take over. *But what if he reacts the way the police did?* she thought. I'd have to go back to my empty house with Jeff . . . what if he and the skipper take down the decoy before we get back—or worse, what if he wouldn't come with me? . . .

Her mind was spinning as the wet wind tore at the spewing spray. For one irrational moment it seemed that her only chance would be to go up the ladder of the lighthouse and retrieve the decoy. *Then they'll believe me.* The Whaler sped into open water in record time. She had planned to use the binoculars to scan the ladder, but her boat, just inches from lurching out of her control, took both of her hands and all of her attention. The furious tide was going out, the water line a good three feet lower than when she'd been in the same spot with the boys. Chips did some quick calculations, intending to bring the boat up from the town side of the water and next to the ladder. To keep from crashing against the iron-clad column would take every bit of seamanship she possessed.

From there, it would be simple to scurry up, grab the decoy, and head for the town landing and the safety of the harbor master's office, proof in hand that Jeff Taylor had carved both decoys.

As the sun disappeard for the final time, Chips looked up at the western sky where clouds had settled in thick and gray. Cursing the tug-of-war with the wind, she gripped the wheel, balancing her body by standing up. How much simpler it would be, she thought, if she were a hundred-and-forty-pound male rather than a ninety-nine pound female.

Chips let her attention wander a final time, noting the startling absence of boats in the bay. Small craft warnings, no doubt, had been posted by Mr. Ransom.

Her gaze ran along the water and settled on her own house. The flag at the end of the dock flapped furiously, but that was not what held her attention. Below it, running, was a distant figure who, even across the choppy waters, she knew was Jeffrey Taylor.

How long, she thought frantically, would it have taken Mrs. Porter to ask Jeff if he recalled where she had put the decoy? Long enough for him to question—offhandedly, of course— whether Chips had seen it, to be told she was out, and to assure Mrs. Porter that she could go home.

The Whaler hit a swell head on, sending icy water against her as if someone were emptying a bucket. Chips was trembling— she was soaked to the skin—and starting to feel scared.

She realized Jeff was getting in the Allens' sailboat!

There was no sense in watching any more. Her craft was nearly alongside the light. With any luck at all, she could be up the ladder, back down, and in the middle of the basin, at least, before he got to her under sail power.

A violent jarring against the hull of her boat nearly threw her into the bay. Lobster pots! Oh, no, now she had done the very thing the skipper had warned her about. She'd run over the bobber. The wind, as strong as ever, rocked the hull, plunging the boat ahead while the line dragged. It had gotten snared on the outboard propellor and was jammed into the pins holding the engine to the stern.

It became impossible to steer, so Chips let go of the wheel and cut the engine, tripping over her bag as she hurried to the stern. In her frantic haste she plunged her hand to the jammed line, missed, and hit the blade of the motor, opening a jagged wound on the palm of her hand.

Chips cried out but kept working, gritting her teeth as she plunged both hands into the salt water to free the bobber.

The pain of the salt on her injured hand brought tears to her eyes. As she yanked on the bobber, the line held tightly by the weight below the surface only ground deeper into the wedge between the propellor and stern.

Chips recognized the marker—green and yellow stripes—and considered her two choices. She could cut the bobber free and lose the pot, infuriating the skipper, or she could haul it to the surface and worry about it later.

One glance over her shoulder told her that the sailboat was bearing down on her at a speed that should have thrown Jeff overboard as he leaned out slicing through the water. Chips plunged both hands back around the line, prayed for the adrenaline heroes always got a shot of in books, and hauled as though her life depended on it. It did.

The pain in her raw hand nearly made her knees buckle as she strained. Her tongue tasted blood where she'd bitten her lip, but at just the point where she thought she'd collapse, the line gave. It moved sluggishly as the trap came off the bottom.

However, it had acted as an anchor, and as it came up, the Whaler broke free and moved with the tide toward the shoals. Jeff was gaining. She could see his hair blowing back from his face, his hands gripping the tiller.

Chips pulled again, recalling that a soaking wet cage weighed seventy pounds, empty. As she gave this one her full attention, the motorboat, tossed by the heaving water, ground onto the rocky base of the lighthouse.

The wire and wood cage surfaced, and her cramped hands reached down to haul it over the side. As the cage fell onto the floor of the boat, Chips saw what was inside—and screamed.

The pot at her feet was full. But not of lobsters. It was stuffed with silver from Snug Harbor.

Chips poked her fingers into the wooden cage, realizing the entire structure was lined in plastic. With sickening speed things fell horribly into place.

The sailboat was slow—slow enough, she prayed, for her to scramble up the ladder, grab the decoy, and start the engine. But of course the propellor was broken, the line coiled around the shaft. The engine wouldn't work. She shook her dripping head, trying to clear her thoughts—nearly impossible. She knew only that she wanted to get away from Jeff and that the incriminating evidence tying him to the robberies lay just above her head on the rusty ladder.

"Chips," a voice called out from the water. "What the heck are you doing?"

Her head shot up, a horrified expression crossing her face as she realized how close Jeff was. She tore off her slicker to make moving easier, dropping it over the lobster trap.

With her good hand stretched out for balance, she looked at Jeff, watched him bring the boat alongside, then jumped from the Whaler to the second rung of Bug Light's ladder. Rust came off in her hand, matching the blood smearing her shirt, but it was not until she had scrambled up to the decoy, clutching it to her, when she looked back.

Jeff stood where she had, on the deck of the Whaler. "I know everything," she called, waving the decoy, "and this is the proof."

The look he gave her told her clearly that he was not about to give up and with the agility of a cat he tensed, jumped, and hit the ladder full force.

As his left hand grabbed the ladder, his right landed on her ankle, squeezing her bare skin as he got his balance. The denim of his jeans and heavy duck cloth of the long-sleeved rugby shirt protected him as he inched his way up the ladder, pinning Chips and the decoy against the rust.

9

"This had better be good." Jeff's brown eyes blazed inches from Chips as they clung to the ladder, nose to nose. "You're covered with blood, hanging up here for dear life, soaked to the skin, and looking at me as though I were going to murder you any minute."

"Well, aren't you?" she shot back, pulling hard on the decoy as he tried to take it from her. With her injured hand, she dangled the decoy at arm's length, knowing full well Jeff's reach far outdistanced hers. As if to prove it, he simply shot out for it and pulled it from her, looking at the base for his signature before dropping it with perfect aim into the floundering Whaler.

"Talk! What are you doing up here with my decoy?"

They hung, suspended like two acrobats waiting for the trapeze, until Chips closed her eyes against the pain burning into her hand. "That tone of voice might have worked on Ryan last night, but it won't work on me. You didn't know I'd seen your decoy up here, did you? Well I did and the minute I saw the one you carved for Mrs. Porter I realized what was going on. You and the skipper . . . and the signal . . . pretending not to know what I was talking about. No wonder you wanted me off the island! I've seen you there myself three times!"

"I wanted you off the island because in the first place *you* told *me* about the skipper and in the second place you can't handle the kind of pressure Ryan Kennedy was putting on you!"

Chips wanted nothing more than to get away, anywhere, but she was pinned like a butterfly to a board by the pressure of Jeff's chest.

"I don't believe you," she replied, far more calmly than she felt. "I even found Kristen's bracelet and no matter what Ryan tried to tell me, no girl with that much gold on her wrist is going to lose it just because she's fooling around in the woods. The police told me the Satterfields' hadn't been robbed, so you must have gotten it from her, somehow."

The combined weight on the ancient ladder tore a bolt from the iron panel making Chips gasp and Jeff lose his grip. In the instant he moved, she sprang up the remaining rungs to the balcony, only to find that even ninety-nine pounds made it sway.

"Get down," he warned. "The whole railing could tear away. Listen to me. The Satterfields' *were* robbed."

"I knew it," she cried, "I knew the minute I saw the bracelet, though I was praying you were only stealing lobsters. . . . Even on my way out here I wasn't sure, not until I ran over the evidence."

"What evidence?" Jeff's voice was cool again, smooth and low as he inched his way up the rungs to where she knelt on the balcony.

"Jeff, I am not stupid. The lobster pot down there under my slicker. Someone will see my boat, you know you can't get away with this any more."

It took a moment before Chips realized that she had lost her fear. Jeff, now kneeling next to her, wouldn't chance getting in any deeper than he already was—not by hurting her. Of that she was certain.

She felt her throat tighten against the tears. "How could you? Everyone trusted you, the Russos, my parents, me. Last night . . . I felt as though you really cared. Was it all an act to get me to trust you, too?"

Jeff looked at her, his brown eyes shining, and steadied her with a hand on each shoulder, tightening the hold as she tried to pull away.

"Trust me once more, Chips. Tell me what evidence is in the lobster pot."

"As if you didn't know."

"You found the jewelry, didn't you? The Satterfields' silver and jewels."

He said it so quietly that she simply nodded, her mind racing ahead to make the judgment that she was safer, clinging here, than she would be throwing herself into the bay—the only alternative.

And then the grip of Jeff's fingers was bringing her roughly to her feet, oblivious of the sudden creak of the balcony. She was cold, terribly cold, shaking, bleeding, but angry enough to keep the fire in her eyes as Jeff looked at her.

"Trust me now, or you'll get yourself killed." Before she could protest, Jeff pulled her shivering body into his arms and kissed her—a warm kiss, so full of tenderness, she stopped trembling.

"I love everything about you," she thought he said as her mouth fell open. "You're crazy and headstrong and the best sailor in this town . . . and by far the cutest."

"You think that?"

Jeff gave her the first smile of the afternoon. "I've thought so from the moment you nearly wiped out on your bike in front of my Jeep."

"You never said a word."

He shook his head. "Your father hired me for a job I knew I'd never get if we were dating. And you've been so wrapped up with Ryan, there wasn't any point."

She barely had time to absorb what he was saying before the warmth drained from his face, replaced by cold calculation. "Now listen to me. Listen to someone who cares about you. I have explored every inch of that island; I enjoy it. That doesn't make me a thief.

"I have never been to the cove with Kristen Satterfield. You saw us on the only date we've ever had because not only is she not my type, she left the next morning with her family. They are camping in Virginia, Chips.

"First thing this morning, I went to the police and told them they were away because I figured out that you were righter than you knew about the bracelet. They went over to the house and discovered it had been broken into."

"But you let me think . . . last night when I told you . . . "

"Crazy and headstrong," he broke in, "remember? I knew darn well if I told you, you'd fly right back over here with a spade and dig up the island if you had to."

"The signal from the dock last night," she threw out.

"What signal?"

"With our flashlight, the same big one you used on Ryan."

"I dropped it on the dock and knocked the contact loose. Chips, I was down there shaking it to get it to work."

Chips put her weight back against the cold, dank column, feeling as though she were holding it up. She shook her head. "I want to believe you. But my boat. You frayed the halyard and then stole it when I didn't stay away."

The sound of another engine made them both look over and for a moment Chips thought it was to be her rescue. But it was the skipper, shooting out from the island, nearly running his derelict outboard into the Whaler in his haste to anchor and scramble up the ladder. There was nothing to do but wait helplessly.

"Jensen," Jeff exclaimed, "so that's who's been scaring you to death."

The older man scrambled up to them, stepping close to Chips. "You crazy fool kid. For weeks I've been trying to get you out of my hair."

"You and Jeff!" she cried.

Backing steadily away, sliding with the grace of a ballerina around the great curving mass to the village side of the light-house, away from the bearded face coming toward her, one foot at a time. For a moment, the skipper looked confused—or was he just pretending? "Me and Taylor," he repeated.

When she could no longer stand the black eyes boring into hers, she blurted out what she suspected. "You would set out one of those decoy sea gulls that Jeff carved as a signal that the loot was ready to be picked up. Then whoever it was would come, drag up the lobster pot, and get away." Jensen looked down at the slicker in her boat, his face tight and angry.

"How could you?" was all she could say.

"Chips, this is Nils Jensen, he owns a novelty shop in Plymouth. He buys my carvings. That's the only way I know him." Jeff's explanation made her turn.

She looked back to Jensen. "He's right about one thing, I buy the birds. Come on, little lady, you don't think this is a one-man operation? You've hit the big time down there in your little boat, big time stuff that takes inside information from a innocent-looking kid like Taylor." He began to step again, one foot deliberately in front of the other.

"Chips, he's lying, trust your instincts, please!" Jeff's voice came not from behind the skipper, but from behind her. He had worked his way around the railing in the opposite direction, approaching her from the back. The metal creaked beneath the weight.

This time Chips stepped sideways, pressing her back against the lighthouse, terrified anew of the enemy on her left and the false friend on the right.

"Come over here," Jeff continued, "and get away from him."

The fear and the pain in her hand kept her from thinking clearly. She wanted to believe Jeff. It was everything he'd said against everything she'd seen with her own eyes and everything the skipper was still saying . . .

But the kiss . . .

Above the wind and the rising anger in the skipper's voice, the siren of a police boat shattered the evening. Out beyond them, a blue light spun on the bow as the harbor master approached.

"Mrs. Porter—" Jeff told her, "—she said if I hadn't saved your neck in half an hour, she'd call the harbor master. Chips, would I let her do that if I'd had any idea what was going on?"

Jeff's reasoning came too late. As Chips turned to answer him, at last thinking he might be telling the truth, Nils Jensen took one look at the police boat and threw his arm around her ribs, slamming her back against him. She was incapable of screaming as the force knocked the breath from her lungs.

"Any closer and this whole lighthouse will fall apart," Jensen growled as the supports groaned under him. "You'll kill us all." Jeff was still.

"Jimmerson!" Cracked from a bullhorn on the patrol boat.

Chips felt herself being pulled in against the column as Jensen lowered his voice to a harsh, terrifying whisper. "Okay, Taylor, go to the edge and yell down that you're fine. The boat ran aground, you were having a look around, and you'll both be right down. I'm a good Samaritan, come to help, is all."

"No way, Jensen."

From what seemed out of nowhere, the skipper's right hand brought a knife to Chips's temple. "Believe me, I'd just as soon leave you both up here for the sea gulls. Just cover me. Now!"

Jeff did as he was told, turning to the patrol boat. "We're all right. We ran aground but we've got help now," he called down in apology, all the while watching where he distributed his weight on the creaking platform.

"I did it," he said in a dead voice. "Now let her go. You can go down first and tell them anything you like."

"The girl goes first." The skipper shoved Chips ahead of him as the sound of his name cracked over the bullhorn.

"Jensen, Nils Jensen."

Chips screamed as desperation made the skipper's face darken and the knife rose in his hand. The razor sharp blade caught the light and gleamed. With all her remaining strength, Chips threw herself against his back, knocking him off balance.

Jeff's hand went up for Jensen's wrist. Someone was screaming. Was it her own voice? The skipper swore and swung his arm, missing his mark by inches.

Chips's last glimpse of Jeff was as he recoiled, back against the outside railing. His blue rugby shirt opened like the spine of a flounder, the blade slicing through his shoulder and into his arm. His brown eyes, drawn in shock, looked at Chips while crimson spread across the shirt.

It wasn't a scream, it was the high-pitched tearing of metal against metal as bolts tore from the iron plates. Jeff's blood-stained hand came up to Jensen's throat. For the blink of an eye, the two of them hung in front of her, suspended.

And then there was nothing. The balcony, brittle and bent, collapsed under them, but all she remembered seeing was the knife—twisting, catching a beam of sunlight that had pushed through the clouds.

Chips did not have the strength to keep herself from falling. When the mesh beneath her boat shoes shifted, she grabbed at air and plunged into Snug Harbor.

*   *   *

She was not dead. Chips was in too much pain to be dead, but she *was* underwater, salt water irritating the mass of scrapes covering her bare legs. Get your cut into the air, she told herself, shooting her wounded hand above her head as she came gasping to the surface.

With one very sore hand, she tentatively touched the drenched face bobbing next to her. "Jeff!" she choked, spitting the water out of her mouth.

His weak left arm came around her ribs as Chips pulled him in with her right. "This is great," he sputtered, "I've always wanted to be saved by a beautiful woman."

Their legs got tangled together as both kicked hard, moving in the direction of the patrol boat. Chips coughed as another whitecap swell hit her full in the face. The arm around her loosened as he struggled to help. She hated to think of how much of an effort it must have been for him.

Chips was still alert enough to see a second boat, a Coast Guard cutter, which was dealing with Jensen, hauling him over the side like a beached tuna. The harbor master and Detective Witter were waiting for her.

Jeff's complexion was as gray as the sky by the time they reached the rope ladder and the boat. "Take him first, he's losing blood," Chips insisted, pushing her hands against his back as the turbulent water drove her under.

Someone was making her cut worse, pulling her hand off ... lifting ... wrapping ... all the while a VHF police radio crackled. There were two ambulances and Mrs. Porter and faces at the town landing, Ryan's face. Then, it smelled like her father's office, the emergency room ... someone was cutting Jeff's shirt off, drawing the white curtain, peeling away her soaking clothes ... warming her ... and then she slept as soon as they told her that Jeff was sleeping, too.

" '... Credit where credit is due.' " Harbor Master Ransome told reporters. "If it hadn't been for Elizabeth Jimmerson the case might never have been solved. As it is, the young sailing instructor broke the back of a major fencing operation involving hundreds of thousands of dollars in stolen goods. Valuable articles from Snug Harbor and neighboring communities as far inland as Maplewood were transferred under darkness from specially designed lobster pots to waiting boats. A decoy sea gull placed on the steps of Bug Light was the signal that the loot was there to be picked up. Known drug dealer Nils Jensen has implicated two Plymouth fishermen in a network stretching to the Rhode Island border.

"There seems no choice but to beg Miss Jimmerson to join the police force so that the town can continue to benefit from her expertise."

"It doesn't say that!" Chips protested as Jeff put down the Boston paper and smiled. "Read the part about the skillfully carved decoys by the handsome boardsailor."

"I'd love to," he answered, "but I don't recall seeing any *skillfully, handsome,* or *boardsailor. You* must have made that up." It was three days later.

The two of them sat propped up on the Jimmersons' porch, pillows cushioning the bruises, sutures, and aches they had acquired as a result of their adventure. Chips touched Jeff's arm as though she still had to convince herself she *hadn't* made him up.

"They also didn't mention that I ruined my father's medical

convention and nearly killed the one person I should have trusted all along."

"Minor details. It does say the Lightning was found in Plymouth when they nabbed those two fishermen."

Chips's mother, who had been sharing iced coffee with Jeff's in the living room, stuck her head in the door.

"Darling, Ryan is on the phone. I told him I was taking messages." She paused and looked apologetically at Jeff. "He'd like to take you to a movie if you're feeling up to it."

Chips's reaction was automatic. She shook her head. "Tell Ryan I'll call him later. But no, Mom, I'm not going out with him."

When her mother had gone, Chips snuggled back into her spot next to Jeff, careful not to lean against his bandaged shoulder.

"Maybe he wants a second chance," he said quietly to her.

Chips shook her head again. "Ryan wasn't right for me . . . but all this time you—I thought that, to you, I was just this little kid who kept making a fool of herself—so I wanted you to think I was sophisticated, that I could be as fast as Kristen. Jeff, I don't have any brothers or anything. I mean, I never thought about boys having feelings—that is, until you talked to me the night—"

He put his hand over hers. "I remember the night."

Chips turned to look into his eyes. "I was amazed that you of all people would know how I felt, that awful achey lump inside. I guess you must have someone who's pretty special to you."

"Yeah, *very* special," he said, looking deeply into her eyes.

"Oh, Jeff," she sighed, "was it somebody in Connecticut, before you moved here?"

He shook his head. "Right here, as a matter of fact. All she could talk about was the high school hero."

"How tacky."

"She even kissed him in front of me—more than once, as though I weren't even there."

"Oh, Jeff, how could anyone not think you're wonderful? That sense of humor, all the things you can do so well . . . your sail-board. Even my students got a crush on you!"

She brought her gauzed-wrapped hand up to his cheek. "I know exactly how you must have felt, it feels just like a knife, doesn't it? Right under your ribs."

Jeff laughed. "Now that I know what *that* feels like, I'd have to say not exactly the same. Competing with the soccer captain is a little different from keeping Nils Jensen from murdering us."

"Soccer captain?" Her face flushed. "Me, Jeff? I'm that *someone?*

"Who else?" He grinned.

The ache was back, filling Chips's lungs, her heart, her throat—but this time, it was from happiness. "Can you ever for-give me?"

"I'd sure like to try," was the last thing he said as he closed his eyes and kissed her.